DARKNESS WITH A CHANCE OF WHIMSY

Ten Years, Ten Stories

R. J. SULLIVAN

Table of Contents

*Dedicated to Robert Alton Sullivan, or as I know him, "Dad."
My first line editor—and a darn tough one. He taught me how to be a writer
and a man.*

Acknowledgments

Here is where I usually present my laundry list of individuals who were especially helpful on this project. In the case of a collection spanning so much time, the list is too long to even try. I'll only embarrass myself. You know who you are.

So I'll take this space to say Thank You to My Loyal Readers. If not for you, I'm just wasting time on my laptop. You make it all worth the effort.

Introduction by Debra Holland

I met R.J. Sullivan when I joined my very first Yahoo group for the fans of a science fiction author, back when I still used a dial-up connection. R.J. and I discovered we were both science fiction and fantasy authors and formed a friendship—my first online friendship. We exchanged our books to critique. I gave him *Sower of Dreams—Book One of the God's Dream Trilogy*. At the time, *Sower* was a stand-alone book. It was R.J. who suggested he could see the story developing into a trilogy. I critiqued *Haunting Blue*, a paranormal thriller with an edgy young female protagonist. I did think he should take out some of the horror elements, but wisely, he didn't listen to me.

When we first started critiquing each other's work, we still had a lot to learn about the craft of writing (not that an author ever stops learning the craft). Publishing our books was just a distant dream, and we had a lot of years of work and submissions and rejections before each of us followed different paths to success.

Science fiction, fantasy, paranormal thrillers, space opera—R.J's talents are remarkable and diverse. After a few years, our writing output grew too much to keep critiquing each other, although from time to time, one of us might ask the other to look at a short piece.

Last year, R.J. invited me to join a speculative fiction anthology to benefit Indy Reads Books, a literacy organization, and it was good to work together on *Gifts of the Magi*.

Umpteen years later, we still have never met in person, but I consider R.J. a good friend. I've watched his career with pride, and I'm honored to introduce this collection. Some of the works have had my fingers on them, others have not. I hope you enjoy the stories as much as I have.

Debra Holland
New York Times and USA Today Bestselling Author

The Assurance Salesman

"The Assurance Salesman" was my first sale. In my exuberant youth, I wanted to use fantastic elements to explore some of my writerly ideas about love and faith and commitment (such as I knew about it in college). So I channeled my inner Rod Serling to create a surreal tale set on a midnight train to London. Years later (and after a few tweaks and tucks) I think it still holds up okay. Maybe you'll agree.

The story has a long history and a path to publication that most people would not believe. Ultimately, I sold it to Jessie Horsting in 2004, who had just re-launched *Midnight Graffiti* as an experimental e-zine named for her prestigious anthology of the same title. The events that led to the story's sale involve a former member of Black Sabbath, a direct-to-video script synopsis, and a person-to-person handoff of my manuscript. No, really.

SHADOWS FLICKER across the walls of the train, visiting spirits peeking in on the doings of the living. All is silent except for the steady churning of the train wheels, the grinding rhythm echoing in the ears of the five travelers seated in the car.

The passengers stare in a dazed stupor, lulled by the train, content in their own space with their own thoughts.

On one side of the car, bodies entwined, are the newlyweds, Janet and Kevin McConnell. He stares at some fixed point on the wall while cradling her in his arms. She is the only one comfortable enough to actually doze, finding solace with her husband, her blond head nestling against his shoulder.

On the same bench as the newlyweds, Mr. Stewart Collins, an elderly, distinguished gentleman dressed in black formal wear, pats the knee of his wife, Lucy. Even with an obvious layer of makeup hiding the wrinkles around her eyes and a stylish emerald hat covering most of her auburn hair, Lucy Collins still has the ability to turn heads. They sit with their backs straightened in perfect upper-class grace.

The fifth passenger, Gary Finn, reclines alone on the bench across from them; his young face turns toward the window, even though it's too dark to see outside. Gary clutches his heavy brown jacket, having found it an inadequate pillow.

In spite of his frequent business trips, Gary had long ago found it impossible to sleep on a train. After a month on the road, parted from April, his beloved wife of seven years, his mind simply races. Soon, he will be home again.

When he arrives, he will undress and crawl into bed beside his wife's slumbering form, and with the warmth of her body next to his, he will finally slip into a sound sleep. Knowing she is once more next to him, he will dream, something he has not done in thirty days.

Gary looks over at Kevin, acknowledging him with a slight nod.

He's envious of Kevin's apparent comfort. He observes that Janet has no problem relaxing on a train, her chest moving slowly with her even breathing, in, out, in... Gary catches himself staring, and, embarrassed, glances back over at Kevin. He doesn't seem to notice.

Mr. Collins stirs and reaches for his pocket watch. Solid gold. He bragged about it hours earlier when they were still talking, when sunbeams shone through the windows, reflecting off the pale maple insets of the car's interior, flooding the confined space with light.

Those same surfaces now reflect monochronistic moonlight, whitewashing all detail from the room—not that anyone cares anymore.

Click; the lid opens. Stewart groans, snaps the watch closed, rubs his tired eyes, and shakes his head.

Gary dares a whisper. "What time is it?"

"Three. We should be in London in another two hours."

Two hours, Gary thinks. Two more hours of shadows, of being lulled by the chugging of the train. Of small dozes, of not quite falling asleep as the train beats out the rhythm of a false lullaby.

Momentary light catches the clear, plastic-coated sign hanging on the wall over Gary's shoulder—an ad he'd read hours ago, can't see now, and doesn't particularly remember. For a microsecond, he sees Janet's pale face and blond tresses framed in a rectangle of ghostly illumination.

Janet grunts, her head jerks, and her eyes snap open, fully awake.

Gary smiles at her. "I hate it when that happens." His voice sounds hollow and distant in his own ears. "I can never sleep on these damn things, either."

Kevin's arm tightens on her shoulder.

She grips his other hand; her eyes close, and her face relaxes into a look of ecstasy.

As he has done countless times tonight, Gary reaches into the folds of his jacket and pulls out the picture from a hidden pocket. He can't clearly see the image anymore—the soft brunette curls, pouting lips, the pink chiffon dress she wore especially for the occasion. His fingers trail across the cheap frame of beaten plastic, anyway. He has kept her memory in tight rein for so long. It's a game of discipline he plays with himself. When he has to travel, he simply puts the photo away, along with all thoughts of her. It lessens the longing during the days. But not the nights, when her disembodied voice speaks to him over the phone, for he calls her every evening without fail. He dreads the word "goodbye," when he must hang up the receiver and face the spectre of her memory as he lies alone in his quiet hotel room. As usual, he never looks at the picture the entire trip. As usual, in the last twelve hours, he can't put it down.

The older man, Mr. Collins, speaks. "Nothing like returning to the woman you love." He smiles from across the compartment and places his hand on his wife's knee. "I remember when I'd have to be gone, sometimes two months at a time, there'd be my Lucy, standing in the doorway with a martini and a smile, and that was all."

"Stewart!" She tries to sound shocked, but she's too tired.

Stewart's laughter lightens up the dreary mood of the train.

Gary, embarrassed, slides the photo back into the pocket of his bundled jacket. "It's not the going home I mind. It's the wait."

The outside door opens. A cold wind gusts through the outer hall and into the compartment.

Lucy starts and grabs at her hat.

Janet sits upright, gripping Kevin's arm.

A bulky mass wrapped in a black, fluttering cloth jumps into the room, turns, and struggles with the door behind him.

Gary clutches his coat tighter.

Black-gloved hands grip the door handle and pull.

A protest of metal; the door slams shut. A man enveloped in a dark, billowing trench coat stands in the middle of the room, looking around the small compartment.

The room echoes with the stranger's harsh breathing. Every feature of his face is covered by the shadow of a large top hat.

Gary waits in expectation, not daring to breathe.

The stranger speaks. "Excuse me." His voice rumbles, a sound that bounces off the walls.

The shadow spirits seem to flee for an instant, returning only reluctantly to eye this newcomer.

The stranger reaches up and removes the hat, exposing a layer of dark, wavy hair. His sallow skin and thin, youthful face stand in sharp contrast to his dark, piercing eyes, which gaze about the room at each passenger in turn.

Janet squirms as his stare falls upon her.

"My apologies. I did not mean to awaken anyone. I tried to sleep in the other car, but ..." He trails off. The stranger shrugs, and the coat shifts.

A quick lift and toss of his hand, and the top hat sails into the upper compartment. Slowly, the stranger turns. He claims the empty space next to Gary and smiles at each passenger.

They all remain silent.

Frequent travelers know that cliques formed at the beginning of long journeys are sacred for the duration. For many hours, this group has formed such a comradeship. The man had no part in that bonding, making him unwelcome.

The shadows dominate the room. They flicker, glide from corner to corner, across the weary faces.

To Gary, the pulse of the train is louder now, weighing him down and pounding in his head.

Or maybe it's the way the stranger keeps looking at him, a queer half-smile on his face. The dark gaze travels from one person to the other.

Gary takes up the thread of the previous conversation. "Yes, Mr. Collins..." To him, his voice sounds shaky, an imitation of his drowsed stupor moments before. He senses a whiny hint of anxiety in it; a desperation to clear the chill. "I-I'm sure April will be waiting for me when I get home, though at——" his voice fails entirely, then starts back up again, "—a-at six in the morning, I doubt she'll have any ideas like that."

Stewart looks confused, as if he has forgotten the previous conversation. Then, as it all comes back to him, he smiles again. "I suspect you'll have to wait 'til this evening for the *real* welcome home."

"Oh, I rather think not." Gary cradles the jacket in his arms. Thinking of April, his trembling stills; the stranger's intrusion is forgotten with his silence. "Right now, the best welcome home I can get would be for the two of us to drift off to sleep together. That's what I want."

"Those moments are always nice, too," Stewart says. "Gets the strength back up for the next time we can—"

"Stewart!" Lucy elbows her husband, which seems to be about the only thing she's done the entire trip. "Your lechery is becoming tiresome," she scolds. "These young people have no interest in the bedroom habits of an old man."

Stewart grunts but holds back a reply.

Janet speaks in a timid voice from her corner of the car. "You like the tender moments, too?" Her eyes are half-open, her cheek once again tucked against the warmth of her husband's shoulder. Her hand strokes Kevin's fingers.

His face comes to life. He looks down at her, attentive to her expression, her words, everything about her.

Janet beams at her husband. "Moments like this, him, and me, just being with him, and I'm in heaven."

Gary flushes, uncomfortable at this public proclamation of love.

Kevin seems just as stunned, and leans down toward her. His lips graze her forehead.

Gary averts his eyes, letting them have their moment. His gaze falls upon the stranger. What right does the man have to be here and witness this display with the others, those who had talked with Kevin and Janet and developed a respect for their relationship?

The stranger continues to watch, unmoving, with no regard for his invasiveness. "Such a lovely display." Sarcasm peppers the stranger's words. "I wonder if they—or you—understand anything about true love."

Nobody moves. The moment lingers.

Gary shifts uneasily, wondering if the man is talking to him. He turns to the stranger. "I-I beg your pardon?"

A disarming smile crosses the stranger's face, taking the sting from his remark. "What I mean is, perhaps they don't understand how love works." He raises a hand. "I mean no offense, merely a speculation."

Gary blinks rapidly in the dark, floundering, compelled to defend the young couple. "Your speculation confuses me. You have me at a disadvantage."

The stranger motions with his gloved hands to indicate the other passengers. "Imagine love as a multi-headed serpent. The newly-weds here are familiar with one aspect. But other levels linger beyond their ability to perceive."

Gary's anger flares but dissipates just as fast.

The stranger leans forward on the bench, reining in his audience as he places his elbows on his knees and folds his gloved hands together. He looks relaxed, comfortable in the spotlight.

Gary rises to the man's challenge. "I don't think that you—"

"I'm merely trying to come up with an answer to your confusion. I'm suggesting that it's possible that this intense passion your young friends feel isn't love at all."

Janet's face turns a deep shade of red. She sits up, pulling out of the cocoon of Kevin's arm. "If you're to dazzle me with your wit and pseudo-philosophy, I'm not impressed. How dare you presume to tell me my feelings for my husband? As if you had any idea how I might feel."

The words hang in the air, trapped in the confines of the car.

Gary turns to face the stranger. Odd, he thinks, how the stranger's eyes appear so blue up close, yet so dark from a distance.

The stranger settles back on the seat, not quite as confident.

One hand reaches into a pocket of his coat as he speaks. "Please, hear me out."

The stranger meets Janet's glare. "You're right, Janet. That was a stupid thing to say, and you're correct to be insulted."

Gary sees her eyes widen at the stranger's use of her familiar name. He can't recall anyone saying it since the stranger entered the car. But then, the conversation has taken such an odd turn, he can't be sure.

The stranger turns toward Janet; his question shoots across the compartment.

"Janet, do you love Kevin?"

She jumps in her seat. "Uh, what? Yes!"

"Are you sure?"

"Yes, absolutely!"

Kevin's arm tightens around her.

"Does he love you?"

"I know he does."

"Do you? You know this for a fact?"

"Yes." A grimace of impatience crosses her face, briefly smudging her pale beauty. But she cannot turn away. "I...know he loves me. He doesn't need to convince me of that." Both of her hands grip her husband's.

"How? Have you developed some way to get inside his head?"

"I feel—" She stops, groping for the words, "—different with him than I have with anyone else. Unlike I've ever felt before."

"Ah." The stranger nods his head. "I see. But that's the real dilemma, isn't it? Your proof is based on feeling. You don't mean you're truly linked to him in some psychic manner, do you?"

Janet's brows furrow. "Well, no, not literally."

The stranger pauses, leaning forward. "Your proof of his love is based on your own feelings, not his. You know nothing for certain."

Janet trembles. "Well, I suppose you're right, but that's all anyone can possibly ..." She stops in mid-sentence, unable to continue. Her eyes tear up.

Kevin glares at the stranger.

Gary tenses. He wishes the man would leave the compartment and just go away.

Kevin pulls her close. "I think you've said more than enough." There's a hostile edge to his voice.

The stranger refuses to back down. "Why? Are you afraid of what I'm proposing? Think about it for just a second. Maybe Janet only thinks she loves you."

"I rather think her reaction here proves her love. Not that she ever had to. And if it weren't for her interest, I'd've thrown you out of here."

"Yes, she is awfully upset. Maybe because she realizes I could be right."

Before Kevin can reply, the stranger turns toward Gary. "And you, young man, what about the woman waiting for you?"

"Don't start on April. I know she loves me."

"Do you?"

"Yes."

The stranger smiles again. "So sure of yourself?"

Gary's thoughts spin in confusion. "All right, damn you, I get your point. No, I can't get into my wife's head. I don't know with absolute, one hundred percent certainty that she's as in love with me as I am with her. But she shows all the signs to me, she tells me she loves me, and she acts as if she loves me; I have faith in that."

"Ah. Well, that may be good enough for you, but what if you could rely on something more certain?"

With that, he withdraws his hand from the coat pocket, clutching a small object.

Janet and Gary watch, their eyes locking onto the blue-colored rose in his hand. Sculpted of transparent crystal, the petals surround a glowing blue sphere. The rose itself would be enough to capture anyone's attention, but the sphere within glimmers with an inner beauty that brightens the entire car. The shadows dissolve in the overpowering light.

"Wh-what's that? Janet whispers as the stranger extends the crystal in front of her pale face.

Lucy Collins also leans forward.

"Ah, it glitters," says the stranger. "You see how we suddenly have the girls' attention?"

The stranger settles back, allowing the fist-sized object to remain exposed in his hand, gripping it by its curved silver stem so that all in the car can see it.

Gary sees the transparent center of the rose cloud with swirling blue smoke.

The stranger shrugs. "This little beauty—diamond, crystal, charm, I don't really know what—is rather special. It took away all my doubts about love." His eyes harden. "It's also why I'm currently without companionship."

They all wait.

The stranger delights in the moment, letting it linger before continuing. "You see, this rose is magical. I don't understand how it works. I only know that it does. I found it on a train rather similar to this one, under a seat, and I was ready to give it to the stationmaster when I accidentally discovered its powers."

"A charlatan." Stewart speaks, shaking his head. "You're a con artist. I should've known better."

"Oh, no. No gimmick here. Although I'm sure you'll think so, at first. You see, somehow, the crystal center can tap into the mind's eye of another person. I don't pretend to understand magic. Imagine, though, an object that can read your mind, find out who you love, and present you with an image of yourself...from that person's frame of mind."

He extends the glowing blue rose, tantalizingly, in front of Janet's widened eyes. As it inches nearer, she bites her lip.

There is a loud chuckle from Stewart's corner. "Of course. And how much do you ask for this miracle?"

"Fifty pounds for one gaze."

Gary's excitement dampens at the offer. "That's ridiculous. For a silly parlor trick?" But his voice cracks, exposing his lack of conviction.

"I'm sure it makes you feel better to keep insisting that, and I can even see where you're coming from. Which is why—" The stranger spaces his words carefully, aiming them directly at the transfixed woman. "—Janet can have a free look. Once you've accepted her word for it, I'll take your fifty pounds, each in turn."

"Really?" Gary says, feebly. "And what makes you think it's really worth fifty pounds?"

"Fifty pounds to know the unknowable? To make faith fact? Isn't that worth fifty pounds to you?"

Janet's hands are already clasped around the folded petals, which direct the light to make her face shine an eerie blue. She looks at the stranger uncertainly. "What do I do?"

The stranger releases the rose into her hands. As she leans away from him, the stranger blends into the darkness. "Close one eye and focus directly into the center. Don't worry about light, it works even in total darkness. The image will be perfect."

Janet holds the rose close. The stem burns against her trembling fingers; she needs both hands to steady the crystal. She can see the center, not simply clouded, but filled with smoky, animated, swirling mist. An actual light of unknown nature within the rose causes the blue glow.

She hardly has time to reflect on this when the mist clears, and she finds herself staring at an image...of herself.

She is seated in the train, as she was moments earlier, leaning against her husband's shoulder. Only Kevin is not in the picture, at least, not his face.

Her breath leaves her body as she realizes that she is seeing through Kevin's eyes, looking down on his new bride. She can see her own face from his viewpoint.

She remembers the daily routine of seeing her own face in a mirror, angry at the puffiness of her cheeks; at the way her hair would never settle quite right.

In the rose, the flaws remain but are filtered to the point of insignificance. She sees herself, all the features the same, but there is an image, a golden glow over her face and body that is almost angelic. A finger caresses her cheek, and the skin—her skin—feels like the softest, smoothest, most beautiful silk she has ever touched.

Images superimpose themselves rapidly over her body. She can see herself in her nightgown on their wedding night, a sense of pleasure mixed perfectly with tenderness. Purity and passion somehow become one and the same, and she is the source. She tries to force the flaws she sees in herself: the hair, the weight, the temper tantrums. They don't exist in this image. She sees herself, but now she is his perfect woman: sexy, funny, beautiful, giving,

Everything.

THE ROSE DROPS from her hands into the stranger's. She buries herself in Kevin's arms, the joy in her sobs tearing from her. "iloveyouiloveyouohgodhowiloveyou ..." Her arms squeeze her husband's shoulders as she cries. There's no shame left. Nothing to hold back, not now and not ever again.

Her sobs soon reduce themselves to gentle sniffs.

The rest wait in an uneasy silence.

Gary chokes up, both over her delirious happiness and at the vulnerability paired with it.

Janet's voice is barely a whisper in Kevin's shoulder. "I'm sorry. I should never, ever have doubted you. I just got so confused. I knew you loved me, I did, and I love you so much, but I didn't know you saw me like that. I don't deserve it."

Kevin hushes her softly. "It's okay. I know, love, it's okay." He murmurs to her until she quiets down.

"Well," says the stranger, his fingers stroking the petals like a pet rabbit, "I trust there's no doubt as to the authenticity of the view." He looks over at Stewart, whose face is pale from Janet's display.

"Do you still deny the powers of this crystal, Mr. Collins?"

"It's a-a trick. It has to be." His gaze remains on Janet, her shaking frame cradled in Kevin's arms.

"Perhaps you would suggest that the young lady and myself planned this ahead of time to sucker you. Do you believe her capable of that?"

Janet sits up. "No, I didn't!" she explodes. "I've never seen this man before in my life, I swear."

"It's okay," Stewart says.

But Gary hears the uncertainty in Stewart's voice and sees the slight trembling in Stewart's hands.

Stewart reaches toward the rose. "It's a trick. Maybe with mirrors."

The stranger pulls the object away. "Cost you fifty pounds to find out."

This time, Gary has no doubt he sees the stranger's eyes flash from black to an eerie blue, the same blue as the rose.

The stranger's voice takes on a chastising tone. "This is not a charity, Mr. Collins. I give out one free demonstration. I certainly won't make an exception for somebody I know damn well can afford it."

Grudgingly, Stewart reaches into his pocket and begins shuffling through some bills.

Lucy watches his actions, wide-eyed. "What on Earth do you think you're doing?" Her voice is little more than a whisper, but more powerful than the loudest scream.

"You get this conditionally," Stewart says; his mouth curls down in a scowl. "Only if I am unable to find a sign of deception."

The stranger nods. "You are an educated man. Your word should have more than a little power on the others." His blue eyes peer at Gary, then look back. "Perhaps Mr. Finn can hold the money. He can be trusted."

Gary starts, suspicious of how the stranger could have come to such a conclusion.

"Agreed." Stewart extends the bills in Gary's direction.

Gary grabs the money without taking his eyes from the stranger. Then he sees it—when the rose changes hands, the stranger's eyes darken. In fact, the stranger's entire form seems to fade.

Lucy places her hand on Stewart's arm. "Stewart, wait. This is silly."

The rose glows brightly in Stewart's hands. When he turns to look at her, his face is a blue sheen of light. "What's silly about it, my dear?"

"I'm just saying, it's a stunt. I didn't want you spending money foolishly."

Stewart shrugs. "It's already done, dearest one. A gentleman's word, and all that."

"Stewart, don't!"

He focuses his eyes on the blue-glowing center.

"Stewart, Stewart, stop!"

THE MIST PARTS.

Stewart faces an old man with sad, brown eyes, slightly resembling himself, but stooped. He hobbles across a large living room, money hanging out of his pocket. As he watches, a ravishing young woman dances across the floor, her long, auburn hair flying as she turns.

As she waltzes by, her hand snatches a fifty-pound note. The old man keeps walking; he doesn't seem to notice.

The image dissolves to another room. Stewart recognizes their bedroom. The old man is adjusting his tie in the mirror. Lucy—actually a woman of startling beauty who bears little resemblance to the real Lucy—lies in the bed, talking about the next cocktail party. A ghostly image is superimposed over his face as the scene continues.

Now the tie becomes a blindfold, covering the old man's eyes. Stewart can see the young woman in bed. Somebody else is with her. He has red hair and dark eyes. They are under the covers, kissing and laughing. She pulls him on top of her; the laughter stops. There are other sounds—of a more primitive nature.

The figures are locked in an embrace; she rolls on top of him, but he now has a different face, blond hair and blue eyes. She points at the blind old fool and laughs, a hoarse, cackling sound of mockery. Her lover fingers a string of beads around the woman's neck. A birthday gift from the old man, she says, and worth a lot of money, too.

They fall against the mattress, ready to finish, but now the lover sports a beard and displays a tattoo on his left shoulder—

"Mr. Collins?"

He jumps.

The stranger leans in front of him; his dark eyes, which earlier appeared greedy, now register concern and compassion.

Stewart realizes that everyone is staring at him; the sound of the train beats through the walls as the seconds tick by. The stranger's hand grips Stewart's arm on the other side, nails cutting.

"You've been staring into space for nearly thirty seconds," the stranger whispers, taking back the rose.

"What did you see, darling?"

Stewart hears the voice of the woman who talked of her expensive necklace.

"Stewart? D-darling, what's wrong? What did you—"

Stewart jerks his arm. He pulls away but then stabs a finger in front of her face. "Enough! Don't say another word. I know more about you than I ever bargained for, and nothing you can say will change that now."

She shrinks back. She tries to speak, but he stops her with a look.

He swallows, and stands.

The stranger rises to his feet, anxious and waiting.

Stewart stands to his full height, straight and tall. He blinks away tears. He has never stooped; he is not yet old, but he's been blind. He takes a couple of steps toward the door. He will not stoop now, either.

"Stewart…" Gary also rises, placing a hand on Stewart's shoulder.

Stewart can read the compassion on Gary's face.

"I thought, if you wanted, I could help you—"

"No." Stewart's voice sounds quiet in his own ears. He draws a deep breath to put power behind his next words. "No, for a while, at least, I *am* going to be alone." His hand clasps Gary's arm, moved by the concern the young man shows him. "But only for a little while."

"Stewart!" Lucy speaks from the corner. "Whatever you saw, i-it was a trick, remember? You were going to prove it was wrong." Tears well up in her eyes. "It was wrong. It has to be."

Stewart releases Gary's arm and twists the handle of the door. His eyes travel the room one last time, lingering for a few moments on the stranger. "Gary, pay the man."

LUCY CRIES, slumped against the now-closed door as the shadows take inventory, unnoticed. The missing presence is felt by all; no one dares look at the sniffling figure.

No one, save the stranger.

Lucy feels his gaze drilling into her. She turns to him in fury. "Damn you! Damn you and your magic! You had no right to come here and ruin my life like you have! How dare you!"

She screams; leaping to her feet, she swings at him, her clawed fingers cutting the air toward his face.

He catches her wrist in mid-swing, holding it there. His gaze never wavers as he speaks; the words fly at her like daggers. "No, how dare *you*. You could have had any rich man who's looking for a sick woman just like you, someone to bury in diamonds and furs for the rest of his life, as long as you share your bed with him. Why did you have to pick one who actually loved you?"

Her mouth is open in outrage. "He...I ..."

"I only hope, after this is over, Mr. Collins doesn't give up on love—as those men have."

She pulls her hand free, adjusts her hat, and gathers up her imagined dignity. "I have to go talk to him."

"Yes, you do." The stranger turns and crosses the room to his space next to Gary. "Perhaps you can convince him to let you keep the Rolls Royce."

She opens the door in a huff.

The wind cuts in. Nobody moves. No sympathetic faces turn in her direction.

The door shuts with a staccato slam. Silence permeates the cabin. Even the stranger seems at a loss for words.

Gary pulls at a loose string on his jacket, waiting. The stranger's hand comes down on the pile of bills in Gary's lap. Gary notes the blue color in the stranger's eyes but lets the stranger take the money without comment.

When Gary looks over, he sees that Janet and Kevin are staring at him. He shifts uncomfortably in his seat. There is movement, and he knows the stranger is near. He does not turn to face him.

"Mr. Finn—"

"No." Gary shakes his head, trembling. He looks back toward the closed door. He draws his knees up and continues to shake his head. "I—I don't want to know. I don't. Just leave me alone."

The stranger nods and waits. The blue light from the rose pulses across his face.

Gary shivers, but it is not from the cold.

Janet sits up straight.

Kevin's hand weaves through her hair.

Gary can barely make out a tear trickling down Janet's face.

The light from the rose glows even brighter now. The stranger says nothing. Why won't he say something, Gary wonders. Why won't he agree? Or disagree? Or talk about something else—

Gary rummages through his jacket, darting his hand in and out of the pockets. He withdraws the money with trembling fingers. The picture slides out with it. He realizes, with both anger and relief, that he is short the needed money.

He puts the money in his lap, stroking the picture. "April." He speaks out loud. "You love me. I know you do." He can see the outline of her smiling face, pink chiffon…

His eyes lock with the stranger's defiantly. "Well, she does!"

Defensively. "She does."

Desperately. "Doesn't she?"

"I-I only have thirty pounds," he says.

The stranger's eyes harden at the news, his gaze falling upon the crystal rose in his hand.

Gary wonders if the stranger will slip the rose back into his coat pocket.

Making his decision, the stranger takes the money from Gary's lap. "It will suffice, Mr. Finn. Even for a prize such as this, I cannot take what you cannot give."

He extends the rose and one note. "The bargain is sealed…at twenty pounds, should you decide you would rather eat alone this morning after you've seen the truth."

Gary says nothing, realizing the cynical reason behind the salesman's gift—the stranger expects an unpleasant outcome for him. The money is in the stranger's hand, and the rose is in Gary's. His breath comes in sharp jerks. He licks his lips, looking around the room.

Janet averts her eyes, burying her face in Kevin's shoulder.

Kevin shrugs helplessly.

The stranger nods.

The shadows wait.

The petals surround a center that now burns brightly in his vision; the mist parts.

FOR MANY SECONDS, there is nothing but solid blue. Then the light dims to complete darkness, almost...except...

A single candle lights the room. The orange flame flickers from a slight wind. There is a woman. Sitting, no, lying, across cushions.

Pillows. It is a bed, their bedroom. In their flat.

The image closes in.

He sees his wife, April, lying awake on the bed and staring at the flame.

The clock on the night-desk reads 4:07.

This is right now, the early morning. And she's awake. His own thoughts interject, reacting to the strangeness of the vision.

April is always asleep when I come home.

Or is she?

But here she is now, awake. Nervous. Even desperate. He can feel that her stomach has knotted. He experiences the fluttering as if it were his own, magnified by sudden distress.

I've made up my mind. I'm telling him tonight. I can't bear keeping this secret any longer, and it is far past time he knew. I'll tell him as soon as he gets home. It's time Gary knows that I've gone to see him.

A flush of fury pours over Gary. He almost pulls the crystal away, wanting to bury the truth, but the furious, betrayed part of him wants to know the rest.

April continues her internal monologue, unaware of the trespasser into her deepest thoughts. In a little over an hour, my secret will be out. Amazing how quickly the time has gone. Gary's called every night, and I just couldn't tell him. You don't break this kind of news to someone over the phone. It's not right. And as soon as he walks through that door, I'll tell him. I just don't know how he'll act. He may even be upset, at first.

At first? Gary thinks.

Again, a fluttering response in her gut. A nervous reaction so painful that she reaches down and strokes a hand across her stomach.

No, not her stomach. Her abdomen.

And then, in her internal monologue, she speaks to her abdomen. Calm down, little one. Daddy will be home soon, and then we'll tell him all about our trip to the doctor. And won't he be so surprised?

And with that, she curls herself up against the bed, overwhelmed by simultaneous joy and sorrow. Alone, she cries out once again to her missing husband, needing the other half of herself, who is always so strong for her. As she tries to be strong for him, as well, knowing when they separate it's never by choice, but simply what he must do.

Truthfully, he has always provided rather well for them. And they have always taken full advantage, having good time after good time. Because of those great joys, she puts on her happy face when he leaves, when she must endure living in a daze—a half stupor.

She knows without the slightest doubt that he will always return. No matter where his travels take him, or how long they must endure their parting, he always returns. She can rely on that. Just as he can rely on her being here, waiting for him. It is the foundation of their bond these last seven years. Most burning passions cool after a few years, but theirs has never burned out. Never. And added to that heat over the years is something more precious than any lost desire: complete and total trust.

April caresses her abdomen. Her pregnancy, already two months along, was discovered only a couple of days after he left. It's been too long. He will know tonight.

She knows that the news will shock him, reel him, for just a moment. Until he realizes that they will face this as they have all things, together, supporting each other in all ways. He can count on it.

It's just going to be a rocky few minutes. She picks the clock up. He'll be coming home soon, little one. Daddy will be coming home soon....

THE ROSE DROPS into his lap. He senses that the others, his companions, are on the edge of their seats. He blinks away tears, realizing for the first time that he is crying.

Janet watches, biting her lip.

Gary tries to say something, anything, but no words come.

He has said nothing for many moments; the others are waiting for him to speak. Janet, particularly, looks distressed.

"I—I'm going to be a daddy," is all he can manage to say. It is enough. Janet squeals with joy, Kevin laughs, and the stranger's hand clasps against his shoulder. And as the weight of the emotional exhaustion settles over him, Gary decides that he has paid enough for the privilege of his own private vision. He will keep the rest to himself.

"I am happy for you," the stranger says, slipping the rose into the pocket of his trench coat.

Gary nods, saying nothing.

The stranger prompts him. "Please speak. I am curious to know what is going through your mind."

Gary shakes his head, as if waking from a dream. He rubs his eyes and blinks. He looks at the stranger. "I know what love is," he says. "I always did."

The stranger nods. "Yes, I suppose you did."

Gary chuckles, thinking back to when it all started. It seems years ago. "And I can support what I said earlier. Love is based on faith. I didn't need that rose. Without it, I'd still be in love. I'd still be happy."

The stranger says nothing for a moment. Then he laughs—loudly, madly.

Gary shifts uncomfortably in his seat.

The stranger stands, still shaking his head. "Faith? You think what you have now is faith?"

"Before you ever stepped in here, I had faith in April," Gary insists. "If I had never met you, it would still be just as strong, with or without the rose."

"Of course, you had faith." The stranger nods in agreement, and then his finger raises with the word, "But! You had faith because that was all you *could* have. When I entered, it was the first time you were aware that love could be proven."

The stranger's hand reaches up over the railing; he retrieves his hat. "Now, you answer me this. Was there any one couple here that refused a look at the rose? Did anybody here say, 'No thank you, sir, I have no need for your magic. I know the truth without it.'?"

Gary opens his mouth to speak.

The stranger cuts in. "With conviction, Mr. Finn."

Gary stops, his train of thought broken.

The stranger grasps the door handle. "I've seen this over and over again. Janet was offered a free look. She took it without hesitation. Mr. Collins discovered firsthand the negative side of trading faith for fact. And I even got twenty pounds from *you*, Mr. Finn."

Gary bristles. "So what does that prove? You gave us an opportunity to invade our lovers' innermost thoughts. You speak of faith as if it's a bad thing and offer your crystal rose as a sort of final answer to love. It's no such thing."

The stranger pauses in his action, leaning toward Gary. "Isn't it?"

"Of course not," Gary scoffs. "What have you proven? True love is *not* a single state of mind frozen forever throughout time. Ten years ago, my passion for April undoubtedly matched that of Kevin's for Janet. And ten years from now, in spite of my best efforts, I could end up like Stewart tonight."

As if to dismiss the stranger, Gary turns from him. "What assurance have you truly offered me? A few months, a few weeks, maybe only a day? Beyond that, I must again rely on my devotion to April, and hers to me, to get us through. And the vision I've seen here tonight will mean nothing." Gary risks a glance toward the door. Their eyes meet.

No longer tapping into the power of the crystal, the stranger's face once again appears pale, with dark, sunken eyes.

Gary knows what price he and his fellow passengers paid this evening. Now he ponders what price the stranger must pay to possess such dark magic.

The shoulders of the stranger's trench coat rise and fall in a dramatic shrug. "Maybe you're right, Mr. Finn."

An odd flickering of shadow and light passes over the stranger's face.

He pulls upon the door latch, which clicks noisily as it comes loose. The stranger flashes his charming smile. "Then again, maybe you're not. Have a good evening, all of you."

And he is gone, off to the next car, leaving the three remaining passengers to the mercy of the flickering shadows and the privacy of their own thoughts.

Fade

Ideas can grow from other ideas, sometimes in surprising directions. After listening to an obscure silly song on an obscure album by an obscure band (featuring my favorite vocalist, Cyndi Lauper ,a couple of years before she became not-very-obscure), I took ideas from that song and projected them in a dark direction. The song provided the whimsy, and I added the darkness.

"Fade" was another story from college (only two of many that survived the transition; you're welcome) that found a second and even third life later in my journey as a writer.

I dug up the manuscript in 2003, self-published it as a booklet, and leveraged it as a "gift with purchase" giveaway to help a Cyndi Lauper fan raise money for her breast cancer expenses her insurance would not cover. The idea snowballed, other fans put their memorabilia up on eBay to help our cause, and we ultimately raised over $1,600 for our friend.

Ms. Mary Kay Woolsey fought back her cancer—an

improbable victory because that was her second bout. She has since fought and won a *third* time. And so, this depressing, pessimistic tale is dedicated to her. Make of that what you will.

The story was eventually published in *Indiana Science Fiction Anthology 2011.*

"ARE YOU SURE ABOUT THIS, Anna Blue?" Spencer Blake gazed at the impressive mansion towering three stories overhead and wider than he could take in with a single glance. They still had a good fifty-yard trot along a cobblestone path before they'd reach the spacious porch.

A seemingly unbroken wall of bushes formed a natural border to the property, meticulously trimmed to an exact height to discourage the curious. Similar shrubs bordered the pathway to form a cool, shady walk to an intimidating entrance.

As a first-string fullback for UCLA, Spencer rarely experienced such discomfort. On the other hand, most farm boys from Oklahoma didn't grow up with buddies who lived in luxurious mansions. He eyed the petite blonde prancing next to him, unable to believe that his spunky, smiling girlfriend of six months had actually grown up here. And yet, she approached the enormous entrance with comfortable intimacy.

"Incredible, Anna. You never told me your home was like this. Everything but the moat. Why bother with UCLA when your parents could send you to USC or Harvard? I'd jump on a chance to—"

"Oh, poo." Her sparkling blue eyes returned his look of love, dampening the abruptness of her words. "Yes, Mommy and Daddy are well-off, and Daddy's an important consultant for the government, but I wanted to mingle with real people, not self-important

CPA clones." She trotted up the steps. Spencer followed her to the polished marble porch, still staring at the house and large, double-door entrance offset to the far left-hand side.

"Quit gawking, Spencer-dear, it's undignified. Now, get ready. I'm going to ring the doorbell. I could just let myself in, but they wanted to welcome you themselves."

Spencer fidgeted. "Fine, no big deal, right? Your parents met me at—"

"A half-hour at lunch isn't the same as Thanksgiving weekend. But this is *your* idea, Spence."

Spencer said nothing, upset at her for once-again interrupting him midsentence, one of her less endearing traits, and a bad habit which had increased over the last few weeks.

Anna pulled on one of her blonde curls. "You wanted to be here, remember?"

He remembered, all right. Anna's parents loved the idea. His own parents—not so much. He didn't want to spend four days without her; that was the long and pathetic short of it.

Anna reached out to the doorbell, looking back at Spencer. "There's one other thing, please, Spence. Don't call me Anna Blue in front of them."

Spencer couldn't stop the frown from creeping over his face. "Why not? It's just a pet name."

"I know." Her lower lip protruded in an unattractive pout. "Don't be insulted. They just might think it's a little childish."

Spencer bit back his response. He didn't want her parents to find them arguing. Besides, they'd been fighting a lot recently—too much. *Is she really speaking her* own *feelings?* But the pressures of confronting his girlfriend's parents were bad enough without looking for trouble. He filed the comment away for later.

She rang the doorbell.

He had to refrain from fidgeting. The more their little disagreements tallied up, the more he feared he couldn't take much more. He absolutely wanted the relationship to work. He recalled the first time he saw her practicing with the other cheerleaders. *Lust at first sight.* But her perky, bubbly zest for life made him pursue her exclusively. Until a couple months ago, when she got caught up with—

The inner lock clicked, snapping him out of his reverie. The door opened to reveal the tall, elegant Mrs. Lorraine Sky. Sudden dryness parched his throat.

Mrs. Sky's green-eyed gaze traveled up and down the couple, then she reached out and briefly clasped Spencer's hand. "Good to see you again, Spencer! Come in."

They both stepped inside.

Mrs. Sky opened her arms.

Anna ran into the embrace with an uninhibited squeal.

Spencer stepped past them into the foyer, then saw it wasn't a foyer at all, but a wide teal-blue hallway that extended along the entire left side of the house. Intermittent windows pierced the outer wall, showing off the landscaped lawn. Natural light brightened numerous paintings hanging along the opposite wall. The various blues in the chosen paintings and prints created a cool, homey mood to contrast with the size.

He stared, flabbergasted. One painting of a large sailing ship rolling in the midst of a vicious storm showed dazzling detail; the oncoming waves appeared to jump off the canvas with almost 3-D realism. He searched for a signature, finding the word "Sky" partially masked within the wave jetsam in the lower left corner. *Anna doesn't paint. Must be her mother.* Spencer turned to his hostess. "These paintings are wonderful. I'm surprised. Bl—Anna never mentioned—"

A deep baritone voice called from across the room. "There's my little girl!"

"Daddy!"

Spencer barely moved aside before Anna zipped past him and ran toward the now-open door at the end of the hall. Her father's face broke into a huge smile. Dark curls topped Henry Sky's head, though his equally dark eyes held a twinkle of remembered youth.

As Anna ran into his arms, Henry Sky swept his daughter into a swinging hug. "Hello, baby girl," he mumbled into her hair.

Anna separated and ran back to her mother as Henry extended a hand toward Spencer. "Hello, Spencer. Are you taking good care of my little girl?"

Spencer blushed but returned Henry's youthful grin while they briefly shook hands. Anna and Spencer didn't live together, but they were well-versed in the tricks of fooling dorm security for occasional overnight visits. "We're doing fine, sir."

Mrs. Sky approached, carrying the two suitcases. "Come upstairs, Anna. Your room looks just as you left it."

Spencer stepped forward to take the suitcases. Henry's massive hand fell onto his shoulder, restraining him.

"Let them be, Spencer. They have a lot of catching up to do. Come, join me in the den."

Mrs. Sky and Anna had already slipped past, hurrying down the hall and engrossed in mother and daughter talk.

Henry led Spencer down the long hall. After hours on the practice field, Spencer tended to think in terms of yardage, and he estimated they strode fifty yards down the decorated hallway before passing a large spiral stairwell and approaching an open set of double doors.

Tasteful antique furnishings filled the sitting room, dominated by a brown, plush leather sectional capable of accommodating six bodies easily.

Henry motioned toward the couch.

Spencer sank into it with trepidation.

Henry stepped toward a well-stocked bar, complete with four barstools. "You drink scotch?"

Spencer hesitated, wondering if he was being set up or if Anna's parents were truly so permissive. He played it safe. "No, sir. I don't drink at all. If you have soda—"

"Nonsense. How old are you?"

"Nineteen, sir."

"And you've never had a drink?"

"I didn't say that, sir, but I hardly think—"

"Well, then, you're a football player, right? I remember raising hell back in my pigskin days."

"Well, Coach doesn't want us to—"

"There's lots of things people don't want us to do, but we do them anyway. Am I wrong, Spencer?"

The last comment brought Anna's perspective on her problems into greater clarity. And just like his daughter, Henry didn't give Spencer a chance to complete a thought. "I guess scotch will do."

Henry poured the drinks into cut crystal glasses and handed one to Spencer.

Spencer forced his best smile and accepted the proffered drink. The last thing he needed was to turn loose-lipped in front of Anna's father.

"So, you enjoy dorm life?"

"Oh, I can't complain, Mister— "

"Call me Henry. Everybody does."

"Oh, okay, Henry." He barely missed a beat that time, anticipating the interruption and rolling with it. "It's not bad. Anna's dorm is just a few blocks away. I help her with astronomy, and she gets me through algebra. Anna's pretty smart…" Spencer trailed off. The one time he wanted the interruption, he didn't get it.

"How're you two getting along?"

Spencer twitched, the squeaking leather reflecting his anxiety. The perfect opportunity. He knew he should jump on it. He might never get the nerve later.

He'd gone back and forth about the idea of enlisting Anna's parents in an intervention to confront her about her drug abuse. But one fact overrode the rest. *She'd feel betrayed, and she'd never forgive me.*

So Spencer answered, "Pretty good, overall. I mean, we have our fights, but who doesn't?"

Henry nodded, then drained his glass with a single tip of his head that made Spencer wince. "Well, I'm sure you'll work everything out." He poured himself another, then joined Spencer on the couch.

Even as Henry spoke, Spencer's mind traveled back to the last time he had to "work everything out." He hadn't heard from her for days. She even ignored his frantic text messages, which *never* happened. Finally, worried out of his mind, he'd found her in her room, passed out. Once he revived her, hours later, she told him she'd dropped out of two classes and was on her way to failing a third.

Then, just two days ago, he found her passed out again, this time with a razorblade clutched in her hand.

From Henry's nonchalance, he seemed blissfully unaware of his daughter's problems.

How can I break that kind of news to her parents? He shook off his misgivings. *At least, I have all weekend to think it through.*

They stewed in an awkward silence, so Spencer transitioned to a safe subject. "Your home surprised me. I had no idea that Anna lives so...comfortably."

Henry chuckled. "This is rather recent for all of us, Spence. I've been an inventor of sorts for years. I have Doctorates in Biological Psychology and Electronics, which finally started paying off about five years ago when the government put me in charge of the SPARTAN Project—"

Spencer nearly coughed up his drink. "Oh, my God!" he blurted out. "You're *that* Doctor Sky? The teacher who invented that psychic glove gizmo that enabled one of his students to push a chair six inches just from staring at it? My psych professor was all abuzz about your results. I can't believe Anna never told me."

Henry laughed. "Anna's not allowed to say much about my work, so she probably thought it best not to even get into it. Her little joke, I suppose."

Spencer nodded, though he found very little about her funny these days. "So the hand gadget, it allows a person to concentrate their mind energy into a sort of forcefield?"

Henry nodded. "Yes, the Spartan 2-B. We put the glove away a few months ago and are trying a new approach."

"Can you tell me anything about it?"

"Let's just say that, after my success, the government granted me a...very lucrative budget to explore the next step." Henry thrust the flat of his hand in a cutting motion, indicating the subject a dead one.

Spencer looked down at his empty glass, wondering if he should ask for another. He decided against it.

Henry sipped his drink. "I have a small workshop in the basement. I fix and enhance radio equipment. It keeps me in practice with solid problem solving while my mind works on subjective theory. There's a big difference between the *idea* of tapping the powers of the mind and the *reality* of creating electronic components to do so. My ability to see solutions for both, I suppose, is why the government pays me so well."

The conversation had risen over Spencer's head, and he floundered for an appropriate response.

The door opened, and the women entered.

"Hello, you two," Henry called out. "Spence, why don't you let Anna show you to your room?"

As Spencer took her hand, Anna slanted him her Cheshire grin, then led him out the door. He hoped she was genuinely happy and not just putting on an act.

"He seems like a nice young man," Lorraine said, watching the two go up the stairs.

Henry took another drink, waiting for her to turn her attention back to him.

"Is something wrong?" she asked.

Henry said nothing. He knew she would detect his change of mood. After twenty-five years of marriage, he couldn't keep any secrets from her for long. Henry shook his head. "I honestly don't know."

She sat next to him.

He scooted closer, his eyes never leaving her face.

Lorraine shook her head. "Okay, Henry. Out with it."

He smiled. "It's good news, actually, hon. You see, I've done it."

Bewilderment crossed her features. "Done what, dear?"

"Well, that's what makes this so awkward. You didn't even know I was working on it. I had a major breakthrough on the SPARTAN project. Something happened I didn't anticipate. I still need to contact the Psychic Research Institute and tell them. But I wanted you to know first."

"I *knew* you were working on SPARTAN, not just those radio gizmos. Now tell me everything."

Henry chuckled, draping his arm over Lorraine's shoulders. "A few months ago, I'd redesigned the glove. It seemed to me that accessing the brain through nerve impulses in the arm allowed greater control of the kinetic energy—but it didn't allow for a direct connection to the power source."

"So what did you do?"

Henry tapped an index finger to his own forehead. "The brain itself. The glove acts as a remote device to allow the wearer to directly tap into the psychic powers of the brain. But since access seems affected by proximity, I thought I should have a secondary device that sits on the head. So I reworked the circuitry to fit into a helmet. I sent the schematics off to the PSI and just this morning, they FedExed a completed model."

"And you couldn't wait until Monday to test it," Lorraine's eyebrows drew together. "You didn't test it on yourself, did you? Not without someone there if anything went wrong."

He gave her a sheepish grin, trying to distract her from becoming angry with him. "I thought—it would simply work the same way as the glove. But it's far, far better than I could have hoped." He stopped to catch his breath, trying to reel in the emotions building since this morning.

"Henry, what happened?"

"I slipped the helmet on in my workshop. Just to be sure of what it *couldn't* do, I looked at my worktable and sent a fleeting thought for the table to lift up from the ground. Only the next thing I knew, I heard a screeching noise, and the table began floating—like you see those magicians do on television—only this table—"

"—weighs over two tons," Lorraine finished. "My God, Henry, did you hurt yourself?"

"No." He patted Lorraine's arm. "I didn't touch it. I didn't strain my thoughts, because I didn't even think I could do it. But...as I thought about it, the damn thing just floated from one side of the room to the other. Controlled by my mind."

"Bu—" Lorraine Sky broke off. Her expression blanked as differing emotions struggled to gain control of her face. Doubt, shock, happiness, and horror crossed her features in moments. She squeezed his hand. "Have you told the PRI yet?"

"I left a message for them to call me, but I doubt anyone will hear it all weekend. And then I've been waiting to tell you."

"I have a bad feeling. It's dangerous. Get rid of it, Henry."

Silence permeated the room as Henry absorbed his wife's outburst, and he fought to keep a tight lid on the anger simmering up in him. "You're not serious. Forgetting how good this device could be for the future of humankind, what about how good it could be for *us?* Our ship has just come in. You can't possibly want me to sink it."

"Henry, please, moving small objects a couple inches is one thing. But you don't know its limits. What if every frivolous wish and desire could be accomplished with a simple thought? Henry, you must know how dangerous that kind of power can be. God never wanted us to—"

"God? *You're* pulling the God argument...on *me?*" Henry stood and glared at her. "You're not even particularly religious. But God gave us our minds and talents. I've used mine to create something special. And I think it's something good."

"Henry, that device is too dangerous, even to leave in the house another minute. You should go down right now and——"

"I don't want to discuss this, Lor. I thought you'd be happy." In the silence that followed, Henry Sky realized he wouldn't convince her just yet. "Let's just think about it. There's still time. There's no need to act on it now."

SPENCER UNPACKED his clothes in the spacious "guest room," which contained, among other amenities, a luxurious king-sized bed, a mounted, thirty-two-inch widescreen television, a marvelous redwood dresser and access to a private bathroom with shower. He'd stayed in hotel suites less luxurious, and his dorm room could fit in the walk-in closet. His clothes fit easily into two drawers of the dresser with plenty of room for more.

Once he'd put away his stuff, he sought out Anna. He found himself standing in the loft outside her door, feeling awkward. He reached out, and as his knuckles tapped against the mahogany wood, the door swung aside. *Whoops!*

Anna, sitting before a vanity mirror, jumped to her feet. She clasped one hand into a tight fist. "Hello, Spence."

Across the room, a light still glowed from her bathroom. By now, he knew that look of guilt and what it indicated. *Oh, my God, she wants to get stoned in her parents' house? Really?*

Anna now flashed an inviting smile. She walked toward him, arms outstretched, one hand still balled.

Spencer opened his arms, pretending to accept her too-obvious embrace. As she drew near, his hand clasped her wrist below the fist and squeezed.

Her smile turned into a shocked grimace as she fought to keep her fingers closed. "Stop it, Spence, you're hurting me!"

No contest. A moment later, four colored capsules dribbled onto the carpet.

"Dammit, Anna." He glared at her as he walked toward the lit bathroom. "How many did you take?"

Anna didn't follow him, but her all-too-familiar pout protruded. "None, dearest. I didn't have a chance, thanks to you. I didn't realize you were going to be my babysitter."

"No, and I'm not your parents, either. But I know where to find them."

"You wouldn't dare!"

"Don't push me." He found the unlabeled plastic bottle sitting on the sink counter and swiped it into his pocket. He walked past her, heading out into the hallway.

Anna trailed after him. "Spence, if I have to spend all holiday with them," she snarled. "I'm going to need a little boost. They're *so square!*"

Spencer spun on her. "Not funny. And it's going to stop right now." Stepping out of the room, Spencer spied a second stairwell leading down from this end of the loft. It descended into unfamiliar territory, but at least he'd be on the first floor.

He stomped down the spiral stairwell.

Anna followed behind, her voice rising to a shrill even while she tried to stay quiet, anger seething through her tirade. "What are you going to do? You're going to *tattle* on me to my parents? How childish is that? Wait!"

Spencer forged ahead. He heard Anna's feet padding on the steps above him. He emerged into a large dining area, with two doors to his immediate left. Over the saloon-style doors, he saw a deserted kitchen, but the reflective shine of a metallic door set into the wall caught his attention, and he stepped toward it.

Anna crossed in front of him and grabbed his hand. "Okay, Spence, joke's over. Let's go upstairs, and we'll talk about this."

Frustration flared with anger. "Let go of me."

"Spencer, please—"

He reached toward her chest and pushed. He didn't mean to shove her so hard, but she stumbled backward against the doorway. He gasped as the door behind her opened inward.

She fell through. "Spence, no!"

Jumping after her, he reached out, grabbing a handful of her knitted sweater. They tumbled into a bright room and teetered on the edge of the basement stairs!

He glimpsed a rail. Clawing the thick, baggy sweater at the neck and chest, his other hand grabbed the rail. They fell together across the stair with a rattling thud. One hand held the rail and the other pulled her to his side by her sweater, ensuring Anna wouldn't bump her head or slide down the rest of the way.

Spencer sat, his heart thumping in his chest at the averted disaster, his breath panting in his ears. He wondered if Anna's parents heard the noise and what they might think if Anna and Spencer were caught here. Realizing he still clutched Anna's sweater in a death grip, he lessened his pressure, pulling her unresisting body into a snuggle. He had just saved them both from a head-first fall. He shook his groggy head. "C'mon, Blue, we have to—" He looked on her pale face. She didn't stir. She drew soft, quiet breaths, and her body remained limp in his arms. Alarmed, he probed his fingers into her hair for obvious bruising or bumps. Satisfied she didn't have a head injury, he breathed a sigh of relief. *Poor girl. She must've fainted when we started to fall.* He rearranged himself on the stairs, and, taking a deep breath, scooped her up and descended with her.

Humming florescent strip lamps hung from the ceiling of the cavernous basement. Spencer stared at a large stone worktable with various drafting and cutting tools scattered across the surface. A small workbench alongside held an array of projects in differing states of completion. With exaggerated gentleness, he deposited Anna upon the bench. He watched her petite chest rise and fall, strong and steady. Looking upon her pretty, peaceful face, he considered stealing a kiss but resisted the urge.

He grabbed the back of a chair to still his shaking hands. He'd have expected the Skys to come running at the noise. *The room must be soundproof.* Anna let out a soft groan, and Spencer knelt by her side.

Her eyes opened. "Ohhhh...what happened?" She tried to rise.

Spencer placed a hand on her shoulder, pressing gently. "Wait. Make sure you're not dizzy."

"Honestly, I'm all right."

He helped her to her feet.

She smiled and put her arms around his neck. "My hero," she murmured. She pulled his face down to meet hers.

He gave her a quick kiss, then pulled away. "No, you're not all right." He yanked her hands apart and stood, separating them.

"What's wrong? Why are you angry?"

"Why shouldn't I be?" He turned and glared at her. "This wouldn't have happened if it weren't for your antics."

"I'm sorry, okay? What do you want from me? I just needed something to take the edge off."

Spencer swore and turned back toward the steps.

"Don't tell my parents, Spence. Please. Just give me a little time and help me."

He turned toward her. "I'm trying to help you. I just don't know if I can keep doing this by myself."

Anna nodded, dismissing the subject. She glanced around the shop, eyeing the tools.

He waited for any indication she really cared about herself or that she knew she was in trouble. Instead she simply looked distracted.

"Y'know, I've only been down here once or twice. Weird he left it open. He's usually careful about locking it."

"If that's the case, we should go. They're expecting us, and I don't think you want to be caught down here."

"Hey, what's this?" She reached down and picked up a helmet made of reflective blue metal from the edge of the workbench.

It resembled some sort of hardhat, complete with a dangling

chinstrap. As Anna shifted the helmet in her hands, Spencer noted circuitry on the inside casing.

Seeing her rummage through her father's private work caused a new surge of anger. "Let's go." If she wasn't allowed down here, she was going too far. He considered tossing her over his shoulders and bodily carrying her upstairs.

Shrugging in obvious defiance, she raised the helmet and placed it on her head.

He rolled his eyes at her petulance and wondered if she'd actually taken some of the drugs before he caught her.

She stared back at him, a silly grin on her face.

Maybe she hit her head after all. He sighed, biting back words of mounting frustration. "There. Happy now? You're wearing it. It's too big for you, anyway."

"But what is it? Is Daddy inventing a new game or a tool to punch holes in the wall—" She stabbed her finger at the drywall behind her.

A sharp popping noise assaulted their ears, and a moment later, they both stared, dumbfounded, at a wide, gaping hole in the wall.

"Oh, no," Anna squeaked.

Nice! She broke something! "That's it! I've had enough." Spencer slammed his fists onto the worktable. Sudden pain fueled his anger. "Screw this. You wanna keep playing games, do it without me." He stormed up the stairs.

"Wait, Spence," Anna pleaded. "Don't go. How am I going to explain this?"

He didn't stop.

"Don't you dare walk out on me!"

He paused, but not because he felt sorry for her. It was time to give her a dose of reality. "All you care about is what *you* want. You don't really love anyone—not your parents, and certainly not me. Well, deal with this yourself. I'm out of here." He could feel Anna's gaze tracking him as he stomped up the stairs.

She shouted after him, "Once you leave, you're gonna want me back." Her tone changed to a sudden plea. "Please stop."

"Quit dreaming."

"Spencer, I said *stop!*"

To his surprise, he did exactly that. His legs locked in place. He tried to reach his foot down to the step below him, but his body refused to work. He couldn't move. He opened his mouth to speak.

She stabbed a finger at him. "Shut up! Don't say a word."

Spencer's jaw tightened shut. Paralyzed, he watched in mute fear, panic surging deep inside, helpless to act on or prevent anything that would happen next.

"Listen to you," Anna spat, thinking Spencer's silence voluntary. "So high and mighty. So much better than me. You really think you can just march in here, try to play interference with my parents? That I'd break down in tears and confess everything to Mommy because you threaten to leave me?"

Spencer could move his arms, and he flailed them at her, hoping she'd notice his anxiety. But she must have thought he was trying to stop her just when she was getting up a good head of steam. This only angered her more.

"You've accomplished nothing, Spencer. In fact, you're worse than nothing. I'd be better off if you'd just fade away, so I can get on with my life."

Pain jolted through Spencer. He clasped his stomach, suddenly overtaken with a burning heat. A silent scream tore at his throat.

Anna sobbed, turning her back to him. "You hear me? Fade! Just go away! You're nothing to me. I don't want to see you ever again."

"No!" Henry Sky shouted from the top of the stairs, hurrying to Spencer's side. Henry extended a hand toward Spencer, but the hand passed right through Spencer's arm.

At her father's strangled cry, Anna turned to face them, her eyes round discs of horror.

Spencer reached out—he could now see her through his own

arm. In mute agony, his eyes questioned her. Then he faded away to nothingness.

Henry Sky stood rooted to the steps of the basement, his hand still clasping empty air. He could see his daughter, her gaze fixed on the stairs, staring at the spot where Spencer stood moments before.

Anna put her hands to her head and screamed.

The primal screech tore at Henry's heart.

Anna clasped her hands to her face.

Henry stared in helpless horror as the helmet burst into flames atop her head. He bolted down the stairs and struck at the helmet with his open palm. The helmet flew free of Anna's head. It toppled over, and the flames snuffed out.

Anna pulled at her hair and sank to her knees, her eyes never leaving the spot where Spencer had been.

Behind him, Lorraine screamed and ran forward, pounding down the steps to her daughter's side. She pulled Anna to her, cradling her daughter in her arms. Her gaze fell on the helmet. She spared Henry a final accusing look, burning him to his soul. Then Lorraine turned away from her husband and rocked her daughter.

Anna's body spasmed, her drugged and overcharged brain short-circuiting. As the blackness of oblivion overtook her, she whimpered, "Fade...Fade...Fade...Fade. ..."

Able-Bodied

"Able-Bodied" explores the line that separates our true potential from the limitations we create within ourselves.

At some point in the late 2000s, I became aware of a new e-zine operating out of South Bend, Indiana, called *Strange, Weird and Wonderful*. Determined to support a local publication, I submitted a few of my trunk stories, which were all rejected one after the other.

Seeing it now as a personal challenge, I started thinking about an original story worthy of being labeled strange, weird, and wonderful. The idea came to me fully formed a couple of days later and was accepted.

So I guess you could say I sold the story when I freed myself from my self-imposed limitations and tapped my true potential. Well, maybe not, but I will.

Police detective Todd Harding stood over the sprawled body. *Today was The Whiz Kid's turn to die.*

Brad "The Whiz Kid" Zither lay on his stomach, brains leaking onto the polished oak floor, a look of slack-jawed stupor frozen on his youthful profile. Inches away, a ground-stone paperweight in the shape of the state of Indiana lay on the floor, the bumpy border of Lake Michigan smeared in crimson. The polished surface reflected a bright red stain—brighter than the crushed section on the back of The Whiz Kid's skull, which already began turning a gelatinous purple.

Ten years ago, The Whiz Kid exploded onto the technology scene, growing a "freeware add-on" office assistant program into a multi-million-dollar computer software company.

Tonight, The Whiz Kid had barricaded himself in the extravagant personal library of his luxurious mansion on three acres of the most secured private woodland just north of Indianapolis, but that couldn't save him from death.

In a few hours, The Whiz Kid would lie out on a slab alongside the homeless vet who died tonight of exposure in White River State Park, worth no more and no less.

The crime scene assistants hovered, anxious to clear away the body and start bagging evidence.

Detective Harding shook his head, waving them off. He gave the study a quick preliminary glance. On the wall, the safe door hung open, exposing an empty metal pit.

The noise of a scuffle at the entrance broke Harding from his reverie. A slender, angry blonde stormed through the door, followed closely by the rookie, Rodriguez—his dark skin glistening beneath the stubble of his shaved head, even in this low light. He shot the rookie an annoyed glance. "What the hell, Rodriguez! I said no one enters the crime scene."

"Sorry, Detective. She surprised me."

Though almost a foot shorter than the athletic woman, Rodriguez gripped her upper arm through the worn, ratty-looking knitted blue sweater draped over the distraught woman's shoulders. Her hair lay helter-skelter, as if she'd just woken up.

The woman pushed at the rookie's hands. "I'm not 'no one!'" she snapped, grammatical structure apparently the least of her concerns. As if fighting a draft, the woman crossed her arms over her chest, hands balled into fists at opposite shoulders, entwined in the knotted yarn of her sweater. Her right hand had clawed a large hole into the left shoulder of the tattered garment. "I'm Lauren Zither. This is my home, too! I want to know what you're doing to find my husband's killer."

Detective Harding, usually the tallest and bulkiest person in the room at over 6' and 240 pounds knew he could create a considerable and intimidating presence, aided by his burr haircut, when the need arose. He stepped toward her and noted with satisfaction how the confident anger soon melted from the young woman's face. "Mrs. Zither, we're examining the crime scene—which you seem intent on contaminating. You need to leave the way you came. Besides, there's nothing you want to—"

She reached both hands to her mouth to stifle her shock.

Detective Harding placed a reassuring hand on her trembling shoulder, sinking his fingers into the tattered sweater. *Couldn't she afford a new sweater? This thing's about had it.* "I'm sorry. You don't need to see this."

She moaned into her hands, now pliant to the rookie's guiding pulls toward the double-door entrance. "Who could have done this? It's so...horrible!"

Harding watched Rodriguez usher the grieving widow out. "Keep the room clear, Rodriguez! Crime team only."

Harding placed his hands on his hips and surveyed the scene again. He didn't like it. Not one bit. *It's too...perfect. Too theatrical, too dramatic. Like a middle school stage play rather than the scene of an actual crime.* Harding had examined dozens of murder scenes in his five years on the force—many more gruesome, a few more sterile—but he'd never before seen one so *obvious*. Whoever killed The Whiz Kid might as well have set up a neon sign flashing "Interrupted Random Burglary. Don't look too closely."

An odd thumping broke Harding's concentration. Annoyed, he turned in the direction of the disturbance, then relaxed when he saw the familiar, attractive form of criminologist Jessica Traster, otherwise known as Doc Jessie, placing the first of several mini-cameras in the room. Following her standard practice, Doc Jessie would position at least two, perhaps more, around the crime scene. Documenting the crime-solving process proved an invaluable tool for her research, or so she claimed. He took her word for it.

As she pulled a second camera from her lab coat, she nodded in his direction. "Sorry, didn't mean to disturb you. Do you think the top of the TV will give me a good angle?"

Harding glanced at the TV, then nodded, looking down at his watch. "Since Brad didn't land face-first through the screen, that should be fine. Dareks checked in?"

Doc shook her head, flashing a knowing grin. "Sorry, Detective, haven't seen him. But you know how he is." Placing a third camera onto the corner of a computer desk, she stepped carefully out of the room.

Harding ground his teeth. He'd put together a strong homicide investigation team. And he could sense that, with time, Rodriguez would learn the ropes quickly and work out fine. And Doc Jessie always proved invaluable when it came to analyzing the mental states of both victim and criminal. Then there was his superstar, Shane Dareks, the man who always managed to solve the murders. Most of the time, Harding felt like the second to Dareks instead of the other way around.

Ultimately, Dareks would prove beyond a reasonable doubt exactly what happened here. Harding glanced at his Timex in annoyance. Dareks was twenty-three minutes late and counting.

Harding didn't know what irritated him more—the man's perpetual tardiness or the fact that his performance was so spot-on brilliant that he'd established himself as the single most indispensable part of the team. Once he showed up, he produced the key to the solution with trained, eagle-eyed observation and a sense of deductive reasoning that often left Harding slack-jawed.

Harding still remembered that first night, over four years ago, when Expert Dareks arrived thirty five minutes into the investigation of the death of Robin Valiance, found dead of an apparent suicide-by-hanging.

Harding had examined the room with a fine-tooth comb—literally—before Dareks drifted through the crime scene. As they shook hands for the first time, Harding stared down at the man, a tiny, rumpled nerd.

"Just glad to be here, I hope I can help," Dareks said by way of introduction, followed immediately by, "Say, old man, have you checked the trap door in the fire pit? Sometimes victims leave warning notes behind for the police to find if they know they're being stalked."

Thirty seconds later, Harding held, pinched between ash-colored fingers, the smeared, folded paper that broke the case wide open.

On that first night, whether he'd intended to or not, Dareks had thrown down the gauntlet. Every case since then had wrapped up in the same way—Harding gathered all the clues, then Dareks wandered in several minutes later, and expertly pointed out what Harding missed. Harding tried to make the best of his love-hate relationship. As team leader, Harding received the credit for Dareks' lazy brilliance. Although, to his shame, he knew he was merely the able-bodied assistant to a man clearly his intellectual superior.

If only I could once—just once—solve the damn mystery before Dareks did. Okay, more than once.

Harding shook off the melancholy. *I'm standing around daydreaming when there's a murder to solve!* The body lay with arms askew, like he'd been flapping them in the air prior to hitting the floor. Based on the direction of the body, The Whiz Kid had to have entered the room from a nearby servants' entrance a few feet away rather than the double doors from the hallway.

The entry and foyer were raised above the rest of the library, with two wooden steps dropping down from the entrance into the room proper. The steps were smeared recently with mud and sets of footprints.

Iiiin-ter-esting. Harding approached the foyer and crouched closer. Now after midnight, Harding recalled that it had rained earlier this evening—a steady shower that started around five o'clock and lasted a couple of hours. When he'd first arrived, he'd noticed this doorway from the outside and knew it led directly to a lawn and garden. He recalled seeing a basketball hoop with a cement half-court set up a short walk across the lawn.

So perhaps The Whiz Kid had ventured outside shortly before being attacked. Except....Harding examined the smudge marks more closely.

The footprints, too small to match the shoes on the corpse, could not have been made by The Whiz Kid. So they most likely belonged to the attacker.

Along with the muddy foot impressions, a thicker streak of mud smeared across the top step, cut off at the edge of the stair, streaked across the second step, down along floor level a few inches, and stopped. The legs of the body lay a good, four-foot jump into the room. A couple of random mud drops continued to dry between the bottom step and the body.

A scenario built itself in Harding's mind. The Kid ventured outside shortly after the rain, shooting hoops. Meanwhile, the thief worked his way across the grounds. He waited until Brad finished his game, followed him back through the servant's entrance, snuck up, and hit him from behind.

Except...none of the footprints could be The Kid's. So that would mean…

"I say, old man, tough break for this guy."

Harding glared up at Crime Specialist Dareks.

"Computer genius falls from pedestal and becomes worm meat."

Harding rose, making a point to glance at his watch. "You're late, Dareks. Again. Over half an hour this time."

Dareks rolled his eyes. "I know, Harding, and every time, it's inexcusable of me. All I do at the precinct is sit around the forensics lab, hoping and waiting for your phone call. I'm certainly not—you know—involved in other important cases that *also* demand my attention. Why do we keep having this conversation? Is that what really bothers you, or is it something else? For once, let's be honest."

Harding waved a dismissive hand. "Okay, never mind."

Dareks' gaze traveled across the room. "So, this marks the end of the great Brad Zither, eh? I suppose it'll be all over CNN tomorrow morning."

Harding nodded. "Which is why we need to get it right."

"Oh, how bloody silly!"

Harding withheld his amused reaction to the remarkably British response.

"What a frame-up job! No real random theft was ever so transparent."

"My thoughts exactly," agreed Harding. "Now, check this out." He indicated the dirt smudges with his fingers.

Dareks squatted on the opposite side of the smears, brows furrowed in concentration. "Interesting. Very interesting indeed." His eyes locked with Harding's. "But enough about me, Detective. Let's see what *you* can come up with."

Feeling like a student put on the spot, Harding swallowed back his discomfort and cleared his throat. *I'm in charge,* he reminded himself. "The footprints aren't Brad's. They're too light and too small. They're feminine. The streaky smears, however, match the width and size of Brad's shoes."

Dareks nodded. "I concur."

Harding took another deep breath and tried to talk out the clues. "The paperweight and the position of the body are meant to telegraph that Brad was attacked from behind and that the event happened here in the study. At least, that's what the perp wants us to think. But he wasn't. Because we know Brad walked outside."

Harding indicated the smudges on the steps. "But...he didn't walk in, because he didn't leave footprints. His legs were dragged across the top, then dropped down to the next step. That's because someone carried him in, already unconscious, which means he was attacked outside."

Harding stood and approached the corpse, removing his leather evidence sampling pouch kit from his trench coat pocket. "We're meant to believe he was hit from behind, here, which would mean The Whiz Kid would not have struggled. But if he was originally attacked outside, it's possible he struggled with his killer." He pressed his fingertips into his forehead in a futile attempt to stop the beginnings of a headache.

From across the room, Dareks' voice reached him. "Really? Why would you say that?"

Harding rubbed his hand across his face to refocus. "It's also possible he knew his assailant. The footprints are small and feminine. At the top of the stairs, the mud is thick and ground deep into the floor. Someone with a smaller body frame struggled to carry the dead weight of The Kid through the door from the outside. The killer couldn't keep The Whiz Kid's shoes from dragging down the steps. And when they got to the bottom, they just flung the body across the floor as far as they could and let him land."

Harding drew a thick metal pick from the evidence kit and gingerly grabbed one hand of the corpse. "So let's assume another scenario. The Whiz Kid is shooting hoops outside in the rain, and he's approached. Not by a stranger—by someone he knows. The assailant is smaller. She gets in close. She attacks him when he's vulnerable and least expecting it."

Carefully, meticulously, Harding scraped the pick under the thumb of the cadaver, then moved to the index finger and along each fingernail of the hand. "Even still, the young man would fight, probably fierce and hard, even against a loved one, once he realized the danger."

"You think it's the wife," confirmed Dareks. It wasn't a question. "It makes sense. And the footprints probably fit her frame. But she lives here. You'll have to do a lot better than that."

Holding the pick up with his right hand, Harding shook open a plastic, see-through evidence bag with his left, then dropped the pick into the bag. He held the bag under the light.

The tip of the pick hooked several dull blue fibers of yarn.

Dareks stared, perplexed, at the damning evidence.

Harding smiled at Dareks' confusion. "I'm guessing you didn't see Lauren Zither before you came here?"

Dareks shook his head.

"She's wearing a blue knitted sweater. She was even picking at large holes in the material."

Dareks nodded. "Well, I'd say that cracks the whole thing wide open."

Harding puzzled over Dareks' subdued response to their victory. "Rodriguez!" he called.

The guard opened the double-door entrance a moment later.

Harding marked the bag hastily and handed it to the lieutenant. "Arrest Lauren Zither for the murder of her husband."

Rodriguez took the offered bag and held it up. As recognition settled, his eyes grew wide. "Immediately, sir. Excellent work." Without another moment's hesitation, Rodriguez turned and shut the door.

"Yes, Detective Harding, excellent work. For once."

Harding turned to face Dareks, taken aback at the hostile tone. "What's the problem, Dareks?"

"What's the problem? I fight through all that traffic to get here, leave important work where I'm actually needed and wanted...."

For a moment, Harding had no idea how to respond. *Was this some sort of bad joke?* "Dareks...we're a team. Your services are invaluable. This isn't...surely, this isn't because I beat you to the solution?"

"Ah!" Dareks shook his index finger in Harding's face. "Didn't take us long to get to *that*, now, did it?"

"Dareks, you must be——"

"Just because this case was an unusually easy one, you're going to let it go to your head. I know what you're thinking. 'Harding can do it all himself now. He doesn't need Dareks anymore.'"

"Dareks, what the *hell's* gotten into you?" Harding couldn't believe this bizarre turn of events. "You solve one crime after another after another, but we work as a *team*, and we get credit as a *team*. So for the first time in over a dozen, I get the drop on you, and you throw a tantrum like a spoiled baby? I mean, you can't really be serious."

"No, Harding, that's not it. You just don't get it," Dareks ranted, turning red in the face with passion. "This is the first step. You don't need me anymore." Still fuming, Dareks made a beeline for the door.

Harding called after him. "Dareks, what are you doing? You're an invaluable part of the team. This doesn't change anything."

Dareks swung open the door, shaking his head. "Actually, Harding, it does. I only work with people who need me, and you don't. You'll find my resignation on your desk in the morning."

Long after the door slammed shut, the dramatic overkill of the announcement froze Harding in place.

What just happened? And why did my forensics expert throw a tantrum like a five-year-old brat?

The door reopened. Doc Jessie poked her head in, grinning. "I understand congratulations are in order, boss."

"Huh? Oh. Yes. And maybe no. Dareks just ..." Words failed him. "I think Dareks just quit."

The grin on Doc Jessie's face vanished. She stepped through the door and shut it behind her. "What happened? Tell me."

Harding shrugged. "I don't know. I have no idea. I mean, I know I solved the case myself, for the first time."

"Did you?" The smile reappeared on Doc Jessie's face, bigger than ever. "Harding, that's terrific! Truly wonderful! That must feel so good."

"I...yeah, I suppose so." He returned her grin. "I hate to admit it, but yeah, it does. Except, you should have seen him. Dareks turned vindictive, he went kind of crazy on me, and said I didn't need him anymore. He even threatened to quit."

Doc Jessie nodded, looking a bit sad but not particularly startled.

Harding chuckled. "You don't seem surprised."

Doc Jessie shook her head. "I've seen this coming for a long time. Dareks is...immature in many ways, with a tremendous ego. The moment it's no longer all about him, he acts like a frustrated child."

"Really?" Harding considered this remarkable insight. "I guess I was too wrapped up in my own problems to notice."

"It doesn't matter, though, Harding." Tentatively, she reached out and squeezed his forearm. "He's right. Maybe you're ready...*we're* ready to go on without him."

"What are you saying?"

Doc Jessie met his questioning look with a penetrating gaze. "If he wants to go, let him go. Don't fight it."

Harding shook his head and started walking toward the door. "It's so odd, though. I just wanted to find a solution before he did, just once. What's so terrible about that? I had no idea he'd take it so personally."

"Don't feel bad, Harding. Don't. This is a good thing."

As Harding reached out to the door, it swung open on its own.

Rodriguez stepped into the room. "Lauren Zither's on her way downtown, sir. She pretty much confessed everything as they were taking her away."

Harding nodded. "Good work, Rookie. Thanks for keeping everyone out of the room while Dareks and I solved the case."

Rodriguez smiled, and then shot Harding a perplexed look. "You're welcome, sir. Goodnight."

Harding nodded. It had already been a long night, and that

headache was coming on strong. "See you all tomorrow." And he stepped into the hall, ready for home, still trying to wrap his mind around his homicide team without the brilliant but annoying Shane Dareks.

RODRIGUEZ STARTED at the departing figure of Detective Harding. "Sir—?"

The door shut on Harding's form.

Rodriguez turned to face Doc Jessie. She sat at a small corner desk near the entrance of the library, her laptop open in front of her. She had three windows on the screen, all reflecting differing angles of the room where they stood. He stared, transfixed a moment, at the look of puzzlement reflected on his own face on one of the screens.

She flashed him a smile of greeting. "Something wrong, Rookie?"

He returned her gaze, catching a hint of—was that amusement? —in her bright blue eyes.

"Yes. Well, no. Well...I think so." He mentally kicked himself. *Oh,* that *was smooth.* Very *professional.*

Doc Jessie prompted, "Just tell me what's on your mind."

Rodriguez pointed a thumb in the direction of the door. "What Harding said. About Dareks. About how I'd left them in the room undisturbed."

Raising a cautionary finger for quiet, Doc Jessie stepped past him. She opened the double doors, glanced back and forth, and then closed them. "Go on."

What was that about? Rodriguez took a moment to find his voice. "Doc, you probably know this as well as I do. Harding was the only one in this room. After he chastised me and told me not to let anyone in, well...I didn't let anyone else in. I mean, I knew Dareks was expected tonight. But, Doc, I placed a guard at the servant's entrance with orders to radio me if anyone approached. And I personally never moved from these double doors. I know for a fact, *Dareks never entered the room.*"

Doc Jessie answered Rodriguez's look with a knowing nod. "I expected we'd have this conversation tonight, Rodriguez." She clicked the finger-pad on her laptop, motioning with her other hand for Rodriguez to come near to see the screen. "What I'm showing you is highly classified. Harding's team knows, but that's all. It's not to be shared with other members of the force, do you understand?"

"Doc?" At first, Rodriguez didn't know how to respond. "I...I suppose so. I mean, sure."

"Look."

Rodriguez watched the video unfold on the screen—recreating the events of a few minutes ago.

Harding stood near the servant's entrance of the library, intently examining clues. Then, oddly, he craned his neck up, staring intently at a spot of empty space, and seemed to speak to the air.

Doc Jessie increased the volume, generating considerable hiss, but also reproducing Harding's voice. "Given your track record, I suppose I can't complain."

Harding paused, still focused on a point in space before him, then nodded, and responded to a statement unheard on the recording. "Which is why we need to get it right."

"What the hell?"

Doc Jessie gently shut the laptop.

"Doc, what's going on here? Is our leader some sort of mental case? Are we taking orders from a psychopath?"

"No." Jessie shook her head to emphasize the word. "No, he's not a psychopath. He's not a danger to himself or others. If so, we'd never allow him in the position he's in." Jessie cast her gaze to the floor, her cheeks flushing. "When Harding tested for the academy a little over five years ago, his profile indicated a genius-level capability of deductive reasoning severely inhibited by an acute inferiority complex. Clinically, an inferiority complex is treatable and not disabling. The department called me in to interview him to see how we could use him."

Doc Jessie paused, taking a deep, trembling breath. "Harding knew he wanted to serve on the force. But his lack of faith in his abilities kept him from achieving what he could. I decided he was worth trying to keep. So...I took an aggressive approach to his treatment."

Rodriguez hugged the clipboard against his chest. "So what happened? You performed some sort of experiment on him?"

"Nothing so dramatic as that. I'm no more unethical than Harding is psychotic. The drugs I prescribed were commonly used for a patient with his condition. But the result was...unique, to put it mildly. Harding's deductive brilliance manifested itself, as we'd hoped. I'll never forget when they sent him off on his first case—the hanging victim. They wanted me along to observe. I discovered his mind had structured a complex illusion. By channeling his brilliance into an imaginary character, his battles with his feelings of inferiority were expressed literally."

"But that's insane!" Rodriguez ignored the irony. Instead, he slapped at the clipboard in his hands. "Forensics Expert Shane Dareks, age 43, precinct five, fifteen years on the force, assigned to Harding Crime Team, precinct twelve, since August 2005. Doc, I was hoping to get his autograph! Now you're telling me he's a six-foot rabbit!"

"Actually, he's five foot, four inches," quipped Doc Jessie.

Rodriquez rolled his eyes. "Why go along with the charade?"

"Because he solves crimes!" Jessie snapped. She visibly stopped herself.

She's much more emotionally involved than she wants to admit.

"Harding thinks I'm on his team to provide input on the psychology of the criminal mind," Jessie resumed with her normal cool professionalism, "and I've served in that capacity faithfully. But my actual assignment is to guide his episodes and to try to find a path to recovery.

"Once the force realized what had happened, and the results it produced...." She stopped, unable to finish the thought. "I've seen Harding crack cases and uncover leads on cases dead-ended months earlier. Egged on by Dareks, I've witnessed, frankly, some damn brilliant detective work. Dareks might be an imaginary demon of Harding's psyche, but he produces results."

"But what about the mental stability of Harding?" Rodriguez shook his head. "Did you consider *that* while you're charting your groundbreaking record of success? Doc, you're feeding his delusion. I've seen Dareks' file myself. Where did that come from?"

Jessie wrung her hands and looked down. "We assembled it, of course."

Rodriguez opened his mouth to reply.

She raised a hand to cut him off. "I know it's unorthodox, but it's also necessary—not only to maintain Harding's stability, but to keep his condition on a need-to-know basis. How do you think the rest of the force would respond if they knew we had a schizophrenic on the force?"

"Not very damn well," Rodriguez acknowledged. "I'm not exactly loving the concept, myself."

Doc nodded and reached out, grabbing Rodriguez's arm in a friendly squeeze. "Now you know most of it. But something happened tonight. Something wonderful."

Rodriguez sighed, trying to control the mental spinning of his thoughts. He had absorbed *so much* in the last few minutes. "What now?"

"When Harding and Dareks work together, the pattern is always the same. Harding examines the facts, and his subconscious pieces together the clues. Once Harding's subconscious deduces the solution, without fail, Dareks shows up and 'announces' the solution to Harding."

Rodriguez shrugged. "Okay, so?"

"So, I've tried to encourage Harding to break the cycle. To make his deductions consciously, so when Dareks arrives, Harding could spring the solution on Dareks."

Rodriguez stepped over to a leather chair and sat. "Go on."

"It happened tonight." Jessie smiled, unable to disguise the joy in her tone. "Tonight, Harding deduced the solution at a conscious level and confronted Dareks with the clues."

"Um...okay. So then what?"

"Apparently, Dareks became very upset. Agitated. He insisted he'll resign as early as tomorrow. I thought such a break-off would take place over time, after several successes. But now it appears the first small victory has boosted Harding's confidence so much, his subconscious is speeding along the process."

"So you're saying...Dareks might be a figment of his imagination, but he might also be in the past tense, very soon?"

"Yes!" Jessie nodded. "I think so. At least, I hope so. Soon, Harding can take his proper place on the team, as the lead detective, and embrace the credit he deserves for his own brilliance. Essentially, he'll have cured himself."

Rodriguez shook his head. "You know, I joined the force to protect and serve and see the bad guys get what they deserve. I wasn't expecting to find myself caught up in some wild psychological thriller. But now it sounds like you're telling me I'm in on it just in time for it all to become moot."

Jessie nodded, unable to hide a huge sigh of relief. "If you'd joined a couple of weeks from now, you might not have even known."

Rodriguez shrugged. "So if you're correct, what happens next?"

Jessie considered before answering. "If we're lucky, you and I will take up our proper roles—as the able-bodied assistants in support of Harding's brilliant detective work."

I Remember Clearly…

My first try at Flash Fiction.

As an infant, he cries.

He cries for the reason so many infants cry in the middle of the night.

"Hush, hush, it's okay, Baby," says Mama while snapping on the light.

He stares up at the big glowing bulb, the "spinnies," the blades of the ceiling fan, revolving around and around, goosed into motion by the flipping of the light switch. Thin, brown paddles stand out in sharp contrast to the white pattern of pebbles on the pale ceiling.

Loving arms lift him and place him gently on the padded table, face-up, looking into the bright light. Delicate hands clip a safety strap across his chest. He stares, transfixed by the "spinnies." *OOOOH!*

Mama's drowsy humming comforts. "Oh, Baby, what a mess!

You must have a fever." Mama takes a warm washcloth to clean what needs cleaning.

Warm wiping makes Baby giggle, as do the "spinnies" and the light on the ceiling.

Moments later, Mama dumps the entire mess into a sealed trash bucket. "Yuck, Baby! But you're all clean now!" she coos.

Mama leaves Baby on the table to change soiled sheets. As Baby lies, secured by a strap and wooden safety rails, the breeze from above caresses him.

Mama returns, and suddenly Baby is turned onto his belly.

To his surprise, something is pushed...back there. "Hold still, Baby, at least one minute," Mama calls.

Seconds later, Mama reads the thermometer and confirms what she suspects. "Oh, Baby has a fever! Poor Baby. Time for a bottle."

She leaves the room to fill the bottle with warm milk and an eyedropper full of Baby's medicine. Baby looks up, giggling at the "spinnies" rotating around the large glowing ball.

Soon, Mama sits and rocks Baby, letting him look up at the ceiling, humming a gentle tune until he drifts to sleep. "Poor Baby," coos Mama. "Just a few more days, and soon you'll be all better...."

Now GROWN, he makes an appointment with a psychiatrist.

The stresses of life blend into a heavy weight upon his weary mind. *Where to begin?* He's losing his job; his wife is cheating on him; his best friend has cancer....

"Tell me," coaxes the doctor.

He takes a deep, shaky breath. He fears scoffing and teasing, though he's not sure what he's worried about. He's already confessing to a shrink! "I remember so clearly! I remember...the alien."

"Go on."

"In the middle of the night...the creature...staring down at me...right through the ceiling!" He wipes away tears. "One large inhuman eye! *Glowing* and looking down at me while I was lying in my bed! It waved four, maybe six, grotesque tentacles around its bulbous head and that one glowing yellow eye!"

He waits for a response.

The doctor says nothing.

"It reached down, lifting me right out of the bed, a tentacle pinning me down onto...some sort of table! Then it did all sorts of experiments on me. I even remember an *anal probe!* Night after night, it returned! But no matter what, the next morning, I'd always wake up back in my bed...."

Do Better

"Do Better" is a writing exercise that, unlike most of my writing exercises, I didn't immediately discard afterwards.

"TOMMY?"

Fingers dug into Tommy's shoulder, rousing him from deep sleep. *Oh, Jessica. Now I remember.* Strange to wake up next to his girlfriend. Even more strange to awaken in a room of near-total darkness. He reached down and pressed against the coarse cold of concrete as he drew up into a sitting position. Jessica's voice, full of panic, reached him.

"There's someone in here. She looks like an angel."

"You're dreaming. How can there be? You locked us in here hours ago."

"Don't be mean, Tommy."

He wanted to go on. He *wanted* to be mean. He bit back snide remarks that tried to push out of his lips. As he recalled what had happened, the anger at their stupidity stung all over again, no less shocking or painful than the first time.

"Lock the door, Tommy," she had said.

"Lock the door? It's an abandoned building, sweetheart. No one's supposed to be here. Who's going to walk in?" He'd pressed his hand against her pale, smooth face. At that time, he could still see her, drink in the sight of her delicate beauty that always melted his heart like butter.

Tears welled up in her eyes, and she bit her lower lip with her intensity.

Her eyes promised an incredible night he'd never forget, but only if he complied with her wishes.

"I'll relax more, Tommy," she begged. "It will make it better."

How could he say no? He walked across the hard floor of the abandoned mausoleum, his footsteps echoing in the open chamber, and slammed the outer door shut. The bolt, though rusted, slid smoothly into the cement slot. *When we're finished, it will unlock easily enough.*

Only later, he found out it *wouldn't* unlock easily enough. It wouldn't unlock at all, as if the latch had turned to stone and merged with the outer frame during their minutes of copulation. Then he discovered that several inches of concrete could thoroughly block any sort of cell phone signal.

But that was hours ago, before exhaustion forced his eyes closed, and even the thought of what might happen once their parents realized they were gone could no longer keep him awake.

Now he looked over and . . . indeed, he could barely make out the silhouette of another presence in the room. *Is there really an angel standing over there?* The skeptical side of him screamed, "No, of course not." *Sure, at one time this could be considered hallowed ground, but we're not supposed to be here. If Mom and Dad ever find out I'd snuck out of the house to meet Jessica in an abandoned chapel on the grounds of an ancient graveyard, they'd more likely raise something from Hell than conjure anything angelic to guide you home.*

But there she stood, by the door, and even in the near-total darkness, she radiated an inner light that brought the beautiful, somber features of her face into sharp focus. She turned, took in the two of them, and shook her head.

Befuddled, Tommy could only stare as she reached out a hand toward the door. The air split with the discordant grinding of rusted metal, twisting and giving way, and the door slid open on its own.

The breeze of frosty night air chilled Tommy's body.

The apparition's eyes met his. Did he imagine a twinkle of amusement? As they stood before her in their disheveled clothes, she wagged an index finger at them.

"If you head straight home now, it's not too late. Go now, and do better." With that, she vanished.

Grammetiquette 2030

Another flash fiction. This one never found a home, though I've always liked it. So here it is as a "bonus track."

"Computer, on. Activate *Grammetiquette 2030*." Lilly Sams adjusted the headphone mic close to her lips. "Open a new file, please. Thanks. Begin dictating.

"Hi, Faith. How is it? I'm comfy lots, thanks. The weather's been ugly as hell here lately. Rainy and other yucky stuff. I'm sure you're not missing any of that, being in Arizona and all, but here in the Midwest, it's just not a lot of fun.

"How's the farm? Did your pap get the pony trained yet? I'll bet you can't wait for your first ride! You must be major-cited and all. I'll have to catch a mini-fly out there when that happens.

"Hey, girly, you need to tell me more about Johnny. How can you drop a hint like that and not do the confess? You little skank-ho. Give me all the juice. A lonely girl's gotta fantasize, you know. Talk to you soon, Besties, Lil.

"End document. Send to net account, nickname, Faith."
The *Grammetiquette 2030* sent the following message:

March 9, 2030

Dear Faith,

I expect this message finds you healthy and in good spirits. Things have been going quite well for me, with the exception of the weather. We've experienced a period of unpleasant rain and drizzle with temperatures in the low 50s, which makes traveling difficult and undesirable. Suffice it to say, it's doubtful you've ever experienced such uncomfortable weather in the warm and mild climate of Tucson, Arizona.

I hope the horse farm takes off. I'm anxious to hear details about your father's training of the new pony. You must look forward with great anticipation to the day when you'll take your first ride. Perhaps I'll reserve a mini-plane trip to correlate with that momentous occasion.

I am curious to hear more about John, the man you're dating. Your tantalizing hints of a possible encounter leave me anxious to hear more, as I'm sure was your intention. Please offer more explicit details in your next response.

I hope to call upon you in the near future.

As always, I wish you well.

Your dear friend,

Lil

Inner Strength

A REBECCA BURTON SHORT STORY

A parent will do anything to protect a child, even during a fantastic crisis. In this story, I explore that idea, plus themes of love and trust hinted at in "The Assurance Salesman," and I think I explore them more successfully here.

Unlike my first appearance in *Strange, Weird and Wonderful*, this one came about by invitation from editor in chief D.L. Russell. Flattered and inspired, I accepted, and this story appeared in the issue in which I was the featured author... and in what would end up being the final issue of the magazine.

I try not to dwell on the implications of that too much.

This story marks the first published appearance of Rebecca Burton, though chronologically, the character is many years shy of the paranormal investigator she morphs into in *Haunting Obsession*, "Backstage Pass" (coming up later in this collection), and *Virtual Blue*.

Memory has a way of messing with us. I'd love to say that, as I composed this, I knew exactly how I would use Ms.

> "Becky" Burton in future stories. But I suspect I thought of this as a standalone tale with only the vaguest idea of how it might serve as a springboard.

BENT OVER THE SINK, Todd Burton squinted to keep the lather from burning his eyes. He cupped his hands under the warm water spraying from the tap and splashed it across his face. He reached for a towel and dabbed at his face, staring through falling droplets and examining his reflection for any trace of Halloween makeup.

He'd showered hours ago, but dark highlights from where he'd traced black lines around his eyes still stood out. The white cake makeup had washed away last night without a problem.

Todd experienced this every year, but nevertheless, he applied the same Halloween makeup and black highlights each season, from the same kit he purchased a decade ago. He only put on the Dracula face once a year. The costume was always in style—black cape with red velvet lining, tuxedo jacket and white gloves, the cool fangs applied with adhesive. Though it had been over two decades since he'd last officially collected candy for himself, he still dressed up. And every year, afterwards he looked like David Bowie at the end of a Ziggy Stardust gig.

Grabbing a washcloth, he wiped futilely at the last smears under his left eye. Well, it was worth it to have this father-daughter time— just he and Becky, going door to door. The Prince of Darkness escorting his Little Mermaid (the perfect princess costume for her naturally bright red hair, NOT a cheap, clown-red wig, thank you very much!) while she trick-or-treated for candy.

He squinted at his reflection, noting how the age lines deepened more than last year. Twelve months ago, Todd could not have imagined he would have to barter with his wife, Olivia, for quality father-daughter time.

She's no longer my wife. He closed his eyes against the memory of the words that still burned in his mind nonstop in the months since he'd first heard them. *"I don't love you anymore. And I'm so sorry, but I don't think I ever did."* How do you answer such a statement from your wife of thirteen years? How do you explain to your daughter, whom you love more than anything, that Daddy has to move out of the house?

Without a fight, he turned their suburban home over to his ex, moving a handful of necessities into a modest apartment near the ad agency where he worked as an award-winning copywriter. Without a fight, he accepted ownership of the gas-guzzling van purchased a lifetime ago, when Rebecca was first born and they made their plans to grow the family to four, five, maybe seven. Now he drove the giant box to work every day while Olivia kept the sedan. He couldn't bring himself to sell it. He still cherished the memories attached to the vehicle, even if she didn't.

Without a fight, he conceded that Olivia should keep custody of their daughter, and that Todd should be grateful for the every-other-weekend deal she offered him. He didn't hire an attorney. He couldn't take legal action against someone he still loved, no matter how she felt now.

And last week, he bargained with Olivia, agreeing that he wanted to have Rebecca overnight to take her trick-or-treating. But he wound up giving up his upcoming Thanksgiving weekend with his daughter for the "privilege."

He stared into his own weary face, his bloodshot eyes (not *just* from too much eye makeup), and wondered how it had come to this.

The telltale electronic blips of a Nintendo handheld game reached him from the great room. "Daaaa-deeeee! When are you going to play the videos? You pro-mised! And we gotta leave soon!"

"Coming, sweetie!" He gave his sunken-eyed reflection one last look and dropped the washcloth, giving up on one more fight before turning off the lights and heading into the other room.

He seated himself at the cheap redwood desk holding his computer and surfed over to YouTube. Becky hopped up from the couch, extended her full five-foot six-inch length (and still growing!)

and kept hopping, up and down on the balls of her feet, the way she always did when she tried to contain her excitement. It pleased Todd that they could still find the simple pleasures of fun after the outrageous drama of the past year.

Todd smiled, drinking in the beaming grin on his daughter's face. "Wanna dance?"

"Yes, Daddy."

He clicked on pop singer Fiddle Dee-Dee, selecting Becky's favorite song.

80s-style synthesizers cracked out of the tiny computer speakers. Becky held her arms out in front of her and spun in place. As she built up speed, her bright red hair, today tied in a tail, streaked behind her.

Todd watched, reflecting how, from the moment she could stand, she would spin to the sound of music. He watched his daughter in the throes of her odd but elegant spin, the colors of her clothes blurring with the motion, her bright red hair glowing. He enjoyed the moment, knowing it would end all too soon. "Keep that up, Becky, and one day you'll turn into Wonder Woman."

She stopped in mid-spin and giggled, her green eyes focused on him with no indication of dizziness or disorientation.

She understood the joke, since they often watched episodes of the old Lynda Carter TV series from his DVD box set, a bag of microwave popcorn propped between them.

"I'm trying to save them, Daddy."

Her serious tone took him aback. "What?"

"If I keep spinning, someday I'll learn how to open the door, and then I can save them."

Todd laughed. Becky's imagination games always charmed him. Her brain worked so much like his at that age. One day she'd learn not to speak so frankly of her inspirations, but he loved that she still shared her fantasy world with him. He pulled on her ponytail with affection. "When you grow up, you can do exactly what you want to do."

Becky smiled, then again raised both hands.

Todd withdrew his hand just as her body spun, and her bright red ponytail whipped around. As her body blurred, she appeared to his eyes a tall, thin candle.

TODD BURTON MANEUVERED the van down the narrow side streets of their neighborhood. *Her neighborhood.* He had not so much as stepped up to the front door in eleven months, but he still often thought of it as their home.

If this was still our *home, I wouldn't be dropping Rebecca off in front of the house and heading on to run errands on my own. I'd gather everyone up, and we'd head off to a movie, just the three of us.*

He shook his head, clearing the melancholy. He spent little enough precious time with his daughter, and he hated when runaway thoughts interfered. He adjusted the reflector attached to the rearview mirror, allowing him to look all the way to the back of the van. Rebecca no longer sat in the middle row of seats. Since the separation, she preferred to go to the couch-like seat at the rear and stretch out, her focus locked on her video screen.

Rebecca caught his gaze upon her and smiled. She wiggled her fingers lazily at him and returned her attention to the game in progress.

At least she seems happy. He pulled up parallel to the curb and stared across the lawn to the modern suburban home. Two stories, three bedrooms, plus a loft—the perfect home in which to grow a family.

Todd sighed. He just wished he knew what he could do to change things. He heard the words, heard the excuses, watched the love of his life shake her head and shrug.

"I just don't love you anymore." *Does that even happen?*

He always figured there was someone else, though he never saw any indication, and Rebecca never revealed anything about a new

"Daddy" in her life. But the alternative—that their life together was a lie from the start—was too devastating to face.

Todd released a deep breath, swung open the driver's side door, and stepped onto the street. His gaze traveled across the front porch and over the driveway. The gray Ford Taurus sat peacefully in the two-car driveway, the usual oil stains spotting the pavement next to it, without so much as a telltale drop of fluid or tire track to hint at the comings and goings of someone new.

Eyes still on the house, he stopped in front of the passenger door and popped it open. He thought perhaps the blinds behind the windows shook just a bit, indicating someone inside had noticed their arrival. He braced himself to hear the familiar voice of his soon-to-be-ex wife offer some sort of awkward greeting from the porch.

Todd flashed back to another time, long ago, when Olivia normally drove the "Errand Runner," a name Todd had affectionately dubbed the reconditioned green van during one of his geekier moments. Settling into the passenger seat, Todd channeled his best Harrison Ford voice. "Firing up the sublight engines on the *Errand Runner*, honey." Olivia would roll her eyes and shake her head, inserting the key and waking up the grumpy engine, but she always flashed him an affectionate smile that warmed his heart. The same smile that made him fall in love with her in the first place.

Now, Todd waited for Rebecca to emerge, knowing she needed a few extra seconds to disengage herself from her Nintendo DS, but time stretched beyond the norm. Annoyed, he called into the dark quiet of the van. "Come on, Rebecca, save your game and let's go!"

He knocked insistently against the solid steel siding, knowing the noise would penetrate her concentration, even through headphones. He listened for any answer.

Silence.

"Becky?" The quiet alarmed him. No thumping of feet from the back of the van. No telltale "bleeping" of electronic noise to indicate the obvious preoccupation of his little "nerd-in-the-making." Not even her usual cry for patience, "I'm saving, Daddy!"

"Hey, string bean, save and quit, girl! Now." Though relatively roomy, Todd hated struggling his 6'2" and 240 pounds of bulk around the middle row to the back of the van. *Maybe she just didn't hear me? Did she fall asleep? Maybe she found it a bit* too *comfortable today.*

Todd placed a foot onto the first step and shoved his head into the compartment for an un-obscured view to the back.

Or so he thought.

Instead of the backseat, he saw a fantastic, unreal image—and froze.

Hovering in mid-air was a large maw of a portal, surrounded by a border of green, glowing energy. The wavering oval gaped open about four feet high and perhaps two feet wide, encompassing what looked like the mouth of a cave, lit from within.

"Becky! Oh, my God!" *What the...what in...*He stopped in mid-thought, uncertain where to attribute this unearthly invasion. The portal reminded him of the green screen effect from *Sliders*, an old sci-fi TV show Olivia and he watched on Friday nights back when they dated in college. Only this portal didn't swirl and explode with special effect chaos but hovered stable—stealthy in its silence.

The memory helped Todd come to grips with the situation, and alarm for his sweet daughter pushed forward. Staring into the void, he perceived yellow light flickering on the inside wall of the cave, evidence of a torch or other light-creating object. He also noted the bulky, indistinct shadow crossing the light, and knew for certain that someone—some *thing*—had emerged from the portal. And kidnapped his daughter.

Stooping, Todd took three quick steps into the van, raised a foot toward the portal in a short jump, and dropped to the stone ground of the cave on the other side. He shook off the rational part of his mind. He'd absorb it later. *Where is Rebecca?*

He turned in time to observe the portal close. He stared out of the entrance to the cave, seeing a desolate, pock-marked landscape where the gaping portal had hovered moments before. Todd scanned the unfamiliar landscape. The bizarre plains and valleys didn't matter. He doubted even the most experienced hiker could identify the terrain. Memories of the sci-fi pulp classic character John Carter of Mars flashed through his mind. *Did I transport to another planet?*

He squinted into the dark bowels of the cave, reaching out to brush his fingers along the cool, stone sides of the narrow tunnel while closing in on the flickering orange glow ahead. Another few steps, and the tunnel opened into a cavern, and the sight of the gargantuan beast standing before him shocked him into paralysis.

Even with the wings folded against its back, Todd recognized the demon's enormous strength and power, barely held in check. As the tremendous, hulking creature approached a horizontal stone slab, it reached one giant, taloned hand to its shoulder. With focused restraint, the beast plucked the sleeping girl from his shoulder and lowered her onto the slab with the care of a collector handling a most rare and precious porcelain doll.

Yes, a demon. Like a badass, black and white illustration from his best friend's *Dungeons & Dragons* reference books from his high school days. A friggin' demon straight out of *World of Warcraft.* Green, glistening skin, a pair of wicked, sharp horns protruding from its massive squared head, bulging muscles along its tremendous bulk and exposed chest, and clothed in a pair of furred long pants —*what the hell else could it be but a demon?*

Of course, in those role-playing fantasy games, Todd usually controlled a well-armored, valiant warrior avatar ready with at least one gigantic sword for the occasion. Today, facing the real thing, Todd stood "armed" with a flip-top cell phone he seriously doubted would find a signal, and wearing a v-neck polo top, dark jeans, and his newest pair of never-stylish New Balance sneakers. *All the better to grab Becky and run like hell. But where would I go?*

THE DEMON ARRANGED Rebecca's body into a natural, more comfortable sleeping position. Light from torches on the wall glinted on the wavy red hair spilling over the side of the slab.

In the flickering light, Todd spied ragged zigzags of scars under fresh slash wounds, exposing angry red wounds beneath the pea-green flesh. The demon sank to the floor, dropping to his knees with a grace Todd would not have expected, given the creature's size. In the tense quiet, Todd's locked muscles relaxed, and he could move again, to his great relief.

A husky sound, a combination of a snort and a chant, filled the chamber, and Todd realized the monster now offered some sort of homage to his daughter. Once again in control of his legs, Todd took a first tentative step, only to hear rock crunch beneath his feet. *Shit!*

Before Todd could speak, the grunting chant changed to an open, threatening growl. In an instant, the fearsome creature rose, turned, and glared at Todd. The torchlight caused the irises of the demon's slitted eyes to glow orange, and the roar of anger literally blew across Todd's face in its intensity.

"Who disturbs my meditations?" A moment later, the glowing eyes widened—reflecting amusement, perhaps—at what the creature saw. "A human. In our realm. Not possible, unless ..." The alien eyes widened farther. "You followed me."

As it spoke, one hand reached behind its back, drawing from a scabbard a massive sword Todd knew could slice him in half with one thrust of the demon's muscled arms. The demon took a step toward Todd, brandishing the awesome weapon.

"Unfortunate...for you!"

"Wait!" To Todd's surprise, the demon halted its advance. "You...you took my daughter."

"You ..." The demon's blockish head cocked as if struggling to decipher an alien language.

For all Todd knew, this was exactly the case. "You are the father of the *T'esh Ka'Rah*?"

The inside of Todd's mouth turned bone-dry, knowing what he said next might be his final words. "I am the father of the little girl you've taken from me." Todd stabbed a finger at the still-sleeping form on the stone bed. *With all this noise, my baby must be drugged. There's no way anyone would sleep through that roar.*

"If you are the father of the *T'esh Ka'Rah*, then you know of her purpose. She is the chosen one destined to lead the demons against their oppressors."

"She is a ten-year-old little girl, and if she wakes up here and..." His head spun at the very thought of what she might do. But to show weakness now could doom them both. "She'll go insane without her mom and dad, and...seeing you."

"She was to be trained! She was to be prepared."

"She's a fourth grader, and the only 'training' she's received besides school is piano lessons and clearing levels on *Super Mario Sunshine*. Whoever you think she is, she can't help you now."

"Whoever I think she is?"

To Todd's astonishment, the demon tossed his head back and laughed.

"I *know* who she is. How is it possible that you don't? Surely, the night she was conceived...the ritual of *Alan'gala*, when you took your life mate in the ceremonial garments. Does this mean nothing to you?"

"What the hell are you...?"

Then it hit him. That weird, crazy, incredible night, over ten years ago, a one-time evening of passion he'd always hoped his wife would repeat one day, but never did....

It was late afternoon at the advertising agency. Most days, they treated him well. Most days, at this time, he'd be shutting his computer down and going home. This was not one of those days. He waited with the rest of the creative staff in the bullpen, while, in the conference room down the hall, the CEOs mulled over the most recent draft of a major catalog project far behind schedule and due to hit the press first thing in the morning.

Finally, the executive director emerged from the conference room and stepped into the midst of the cubicle cluster of graphic artists and writers. With a grim look of disgust on his face, he dropped the paperclipped, forty-page printout in the middle of the table with a thump.

Creatively drained, Todd and the rest of the staff waited as executive Randall Whitehead spoke "It needs a redesign, top to bottom. We left notes in the margins. You are all to stay and redesign the catalog for as long as it takes. See you in the morning." Without waiting for a reply, The Big Zit, as the bullpen dubbed him, turned his back and strode toward the exit.

Art Director Barry Watson—Todd's supervisor—rose from his cubicle, released a pent-up sigh, and shook his head as he gathered pages. "Thanks for the warning," he said into the air. "Okay, people, you heard the man. Chris and Todd, here's the first five pages. Chris, you're on redesign. And Todd, start working your magic with the words. Arlo, make fresh coffee. Carley, dig up those pizza coupons." Barry shook his head while his team burst into activity around him. "Everyone email me your favorite toppings. We're pulling an all-nighter."

<hr>

Late in the evening, Todd stared at the computer, fingers flying over the keyboard as his brain condensed the top three reasons for customers to buy moisture-absorbent fitness tops into two lines of hopefully compelling catalog copy.

The phone rang. "Honey, it's 10:30. Are you close to finishing up?" Todd heard the expected concern in Olivia's voice, but something sounded strange.

"Sorry, Liv. At the rate things are going, we're likely to be here until morning. Bad enough I have to rewrite this imbecile's copy, but I'm the proofreader, too, so I have to review the pages once the artists lay them out—"

"But I need to see you tonight."

Todd smiled into the receiver. "Aww, that's sweet. I miss you, too, but—"

"No, I really *need* to be with you tonight. Soon. Before midnight. Can you break away for an hour and come home?"

"I…" The sexy tone in Olivia's voice caused him to flounder. In their seven years of marriage, Olivia had wonderfully needy moments, but historically, she wasn't prone to red-alert booty calls. *What's going on, and why* now?

He shrugged, and then mentally kicked himself when he realized she couldn't see his action. "Liv, I don't think it's possible. They're all counting on me, and—"

"If you can break away for about an hour, I will *so* make it worth your while."

The huskiness in her voice caused a responsive tightening in his groin. Todd looked around the room. Intent on their own business, his co-workers stared into their individual computer screens, oblivious to his conversation.

"Please, Todd. I need you."

"I'll see what I can do."

SLIPPING AWAY PROVED EASIER than he thought. He asked Barry for an hour away to get some fresh air and a quick bite to eat, saying he needed to clear his head for a while.

Barry nodded, his attention still focused on his own screen. "Go on. We'll be building these pages for at least the next two hours, anyway. I don't need you burned out before early morning when you're proofreading." Barry's gaze drifted his direction a moment before returning to the project on the screen. "And if you're going to snort something, don't tell me about it."

"Whatever." Todd waved a hand in his direction and headed toward the door.

———

TEN MINUTES LATER, Todd stepped into his house, dark except for the flickering glow of candlelight dancing from under the crack of the closed bedroom door. He entered the bedroom to a vision of his wife, lying on the bed, several amber-colored flower petals sprinkled beneath her body. In the glow of dozens of candles reflecting off her full curves, Olivia sat up on her elbows, her body bound in an exotic, pearl-white leather corset, a collar circling her neck, and a provocative smile on her luscious red lips. His gaze traced the x-lacing up the front of the sexy garment to where the tops of her breasts strained over the material, wanting release from the restrictive halter.

He lingered over the high hip cut of the garment, down the garters to the fishnet stockings, finished with a pair of high-heeled, white leather Emma Peel boots, as his mind referred to them. He'd never seen the naughty-wear before, but he liked it!

Olivia's blue eyes sparkled with desire.

Todd's gaze fell, momentarily, on the odd pendant adorning the choker collar. Some sort of diamond etched into the shape of a cross. As the pendant caught the candlelight, he tried to bring it into greater focus.

Then Olivia beckoned with one red-tipped finger and issued a throaty, "Get over here, right now!"

He forgot about the pendant for the next ten years.

Who are you, and what have you done with my wife?

On second thought, I'd better just go with this.

Todd took a few tentative steps toward the bed, feeling for the first time since...well, their first time...like a fumbling boy. The scent of cinnamon and rose petals drifted to his senses and rushed to his head, and the room lost focus. He turned and sat on the edge of the bed in what he hoped projected sexual confidence, but his legs had turned rubbery, and he had to lie down.

Olivia leaned over him, pressing her body against his chest, pulling his face towards her and muttering exotic, passionate whisperings in his ear—words he couldn't quite make out. Then, as her hand traveled across his stomach and between his legs, the odd chant became another detail lost for over a decade.

The first burning kiss caused flames of responsive desire to rise within him, and he gladly gave in to her intoxicating powers. She stripped off his clothes, and his love and desire for her rose to new heights. Olivia straddled him, grinding her hot, electrified body over his. Tears of joy streaked her face. Then she leaned close to his ear. "I love you *so* much. Now, time for me to make it worth your while."

And she did.

Though he wasn't exactly a math genius, it didn't take Todd long to subtract nine months from Rebecca's birth date and realize the night she must have been conceived. And over time, it made perfect sense to attribute Olivia's behavior to a womanly instinct or hormonal calling not yet documented by science, but which Todd assumed might be common behavior when a woman is ready to conceive her first child. And except for wishing he knew how to trigger the encounter again, he gave it little thought afterwards.

But now, standing in a cave and trying to rescue his daughter from a demon zealot claiming her birth was carefully calculated and predestined, the most confusing elements of that long-ago encounter took on greater meaning. "Look—I don't know what she's destined to do in the future, but right now, today, I'm telling you, my little girl's not able to help you." Todd kept talking, working his way around the demon to put himself between it and little Becky.

The demon—to be fair—allowed him to do it. Todd sensed the demon could reduce him to a bloody blotch on the wall with a casual swipe of its hand. Todd reached his daughter only because it amused the creature to let him.

The demon spoke with bored nonchalance. "I have no desire to kill the father of the *T'esh Ka'Rah*."

"That's good, because I have no desire to be killed by you." *Stop it, Todd. An attitude will end up getting you killed. You're not Peter Parker. Damn those* Spider-Man *comic books, anyway.* He stood, shoulders back, stance firm, staring face to...ribcage with a giant gargoyle who scoffed at his display of bravado with contempt. Todd felt the gulp of fear in his throat. "Let's just calm down and talk this over."

"For thirty thousand years, I remained calm, and always the soldiers of the Light told us to wait." The demon's response built into a defiant roar. "While the Master's whip tears fresh lashes over ancient scars, my people wait. While the chosen one practices her piano instrument and memorizes her math tables, the Master presses hot brands into our heels because our screams of torment amuse him. And we're told to wait—to be patient. I will wait no longer!"

The demon's screech splashed slime in Todd's face. He didn't dare react.

The demon slammed his hand against the stone wall behind him.

The thump echoed through the chamber, making Todd flinch.

"My patience has ended! Free me!"

Todd reeled from the onslaught, his hip brushing against the stone bed that looked too much like a sacrificial altar for comfort. His composure slipped, and he dropped to his knees, overwhelmed with spasms of fear. "I...can't...help you." He could feel his legs under him again and stood. "And neither can my daughter."

"I will not harm her. You have my word. I would never betray the *T'esh Ka'Rah* or her father."

"Yeah, well, guess what? You already did, when you took her from me." With a surge of courage, Todd turned his back on the creature to look down upon his daughter's delicate form, still deep asleep. *What the hell did he drug you with, my sweet?* Gently, Todd wiggled one arm under her shoulders and the other behind her knees. He turned toward the monster, cradling Becky in his arms and against his chest.

The demon stood erect, towering over him, bringing his sword forward between them.

The menace reflected in the monster's evil red eyes froze Todd's blood.

"I will not let you leave with her!"

Todd drew a deep, shuddering breath. "Then when she wakes up, the first thing you'll need to explain to her is why her father's body is in bloody pieces on the floor. Then see how quick she is to help you." Todd waited, in perhaps the most outrageous standoff of all time, while the demon snarled defiance.

The monster lowered its weapon for just a moment before bringing it up again. "Thousands of years of torture and torment! Can you imagine such a thing, human?"

"No," Todd conceded, wondering at these twinges of sympathy toward the beast that stole his daughter from him. "But I can tell you this: I won't allow you to harm one hair on my little girl while I'm still alive. And after I'm dead, all the pain and misery you might inflict on her will do you no good at all. She's not who you're looking for."

"I would never...I would not...." With a tremendous sigh, the demon lowered its weapon. "You don't understand."

"No, I don't, and as scared as I am, I can promise you, if Becky wakes up down here, I won't be the most hysterical person you'll have to deal with. Let us go!" Todd took a first step toward the hall.

The demon moved to block his path.

Todd looked up into the creature's eyes. *"Please...let us go. Please."* Todd waited, closing his eyes in anticipation of a blow that never came. He sensed, rather than saw, the behemoth take one huge step to the side. "I will restore the portal briefly. Hurry."

Todd could already feel his shaking legs threatening to give out. Without answering, he took fast, awkward strides into the darkened hallway. He plunged into blackness, chased by the sorrowful cries of the damned.

<hr>

As soon as he'd lowered Rebecca's still-limp body onto the back-seat, his legs turned to rubber. The shakes overtook him, and he collapsed onto the carpeted floor of the van. He was still trying to control his own breathing when comforting arms wrapped around him.

His wife spoke in his ear. "It's okay, you're okay. You're both okay. Settle down, Todd. Be at peace."

With those words, the constriction in his chest eased, and the jumbled mess of his thoughts settled themselves, and for the first time in several months, he enjoyed the simple pleasure of Olivia's embrace.

Then she pulled away from him. He cursed his weakness, his perpetual need for her, even after how she'd treated him. But now calm, he sat up, huddled on the floor, and tried to sort through the incredible, impossible information overload.

His daughter...Rebecca...sweet Becky, his innocent child, would somehow grow up to willingly join forces with fearsome creatures. It made no sense. And Olivia...his college sweetheart, the woman he'd trusted unconditionally and who later betrayed that trust. *How deep does that betrayal go?*

Olivia watched him from across the van. "I was afraid the demons would try something like that. So desperate. So stupid. I should never have let you have Rebecca."

Todd glared at her, growing immune to the stack of revelations. "You knew about the demons?"

Her cheeks flared. Her blue-eyed gaze looked away while her face rivaled the flush of her dark red hair.

"What is this about? Helping demons?" It sounded ludicrous in his ears. Until he'd seen them himself, he'd have doubted their very existence beyond the images created by the imaginations of his favorite fantasy artists. "What sort of sickness have you brought my daughter into?"

"Todd, no." Her hands clamped either side of his face, and she stared into his eyes.

Her touch, normally so comforting, burned now, and he tried to pull away.

She met his angry gaze with a pleading one of her own. "Have I kept things from you? Yes. But you *know* me, you know my heart, and you know your daughter's heart. Don't doubt what you know about us."

Todd grabbed her hands and thrust them away. "I *thought* I knew you, Liv! Then a year ago you said you never loved me, and you kicked me out of my home. That's what I know."

She looked back at the floor. The shame on her face was clear. And, God help him, it thrilled him to see her suffer. These few moments could in no way make up for what he'd endured the previous months, but it was a start. "What I also know is that I had to negotiate for the release of our daughter from a ten-foot demon that was way too presumptuous about a future alliance. *My* sweet, innocent child."

Olivia flinched.

A hollow victory, but he would take it. "What do you intend to turn her into?"

"Todd, I—"

"Answer me!"

"I'm trying to!" Her eyes squeezed shut, and tears streaked down her face.

In spite of his anger, he couldn't ignore his surge of deep affection for her, even now. "Go ahead."

"Our daughter is much more than you ever knew. *I'm* much more than you ever knew. Over time, I realized we were in great danger—all of us." She hesitated, swiping the back of her hand across her cheeks in a futile attempt to ebb the tears trickling down her face. "I thought...that it would be impossible for me to protect her if I had to protect *you*, too."

"So you threw me out, you turned my world upside down, you took away everything and everyone that mattered most...to protect me? Is that really what—?"

"I love you, Todd. I never stopped."

Her words stopped him cold. The words he longed to hear but thought he'd never hear again, and the pain seared worse than her denial of that love months earlier.

"When I realized I couldn't protect you, I tried to lie, I tried to make you hate me. I wanted to get you to leave and never want to come back. I thought making you leave was the only way I could be certain you wouldn't be hurt, or even killed."

"Bitch!" Todd closed his eyes against pent-up fury. "How can you sit there now and say you loved me?" After all that happened, he'd never so much as yelled at her until now. Through all the painful changes and her insufferable demands, he'd never fought her.

"I only wanted you safe. You can believe that or not." Olivia shrugged and turned toward the still-slumbering Rebecca. "I have no excuse for what I did. I can't undo it. I'm powerful, but I'm not *that* powerful. And I'm nowhere near as powerful as what our daughter will become when she grows up."

Incredulous, Todd watched his wife of over a decade wave her hands at their daughter's prone body. A green aura traveled from Becky's delicate head to her slackened feet. The air crackled with a brief hiss.

Becky's eyes fluttered open. She looked refreshed and smiling. "Hi, Mommy! Hi, Daddy."

Olivia smiled through tears. "Hello, sweetie."

Becky sat up and fell forward into her mother's open arms.

"Did you have a good nap?" Olivia asked.

"Yes, Mommy. Why are you crying?"

Olivia shook her head, unable to stop a burst of laughter in her relief. "It's nothing, sweetie, I'm just so glad to see you."

Becky stepped up to Todd and wrapped her arms around his neck. "Goodbye, Daddy!" She kissed his cheek. "I guess I'll see you soon?"

Todd swallowed back a lump as he ran his hand over her hair, drinking in the smell of her. "I hope so."

"Go on inside, Becky, I'll be right there," said Olivia.

Numb, Todd heard Becky bolt out the door, then watched through the tinted van window as their daughter darted toward the house and disappeared behind the door.

A sob broke the silence.

Todd stared, amazed, at the sight of his wife crying freely into her hands.

Olivia found her voice. "Thank you, Todd, *so much*, for saving our daughter today."

Todd snapped, "I didn't need convincing to protect our daughter, Liv."

"She's our daughter, and so much more. If we can keep her safe a few more years, one day, she'll save all of us."

Todd shook his head at yet another cryptic comment to add to the mix.

Olivia rose, looking down upon her husband with profound sadness. "You never gave up on me; you never gave up on *us*. You wanted to know why all this was happening." She spread her arms out before her, as if embracing the entire crazy scenario. "I was wrong, and now I have nothing left to hide. If you never want speak to me again, I don't blame you. You will have...fair access to Becky from now on." She worked her way to the front of the van and opened the door, pausing before she stepped outside. "But if you want, you can come into the house and be with your family."

Todd struggled to his feet. "Just like that?" He shook his head. "You withheld your love, you withheld my daughter, for over a year, and just like that, you want me to just come home?"

Olivia stared down at the ground. "No, I want you to come into the house. And...we can go from there." Olivia shut the door.

Todd slapped his hand against the plastic interior of the van. "Shit!" The sting ran through his body and sobered his thoughts. This woman had betrayed him, lied to him, and taken so much from him.

Todd opened the door and stepped into the sunlight. The brightness irritated him, and he slammed his hand against the metal side. The fresh pain traveled up his arm. "Shit!" A stream of profanities poured from his mouth. *Can someone be so cruel to someone they love? Do I want to know?*

Several minutes ago, he'd stared down a towering demon to save his daughter. Walking through the closed door before him now took far more courage.

He always knew, deep down , his wife and child were special. Now he knew Olivia was some sort of mystical sorceress, and Rebecca would one day save the world. So he had that going for him.

Todd shook his head and laughed. If he could still see the bright side in this preposterous situation, he knew what he had to do.

Swallowing back fear, Todd stepped into the grass and approached the closed door where his family waited for him on the other side.

Backstage Pass

A REBECCA BURTON SHORT STORY

"Backstage Pass" explores the fandom/Idol mindset and how extreme fans can often disconnect from reality. Here, a follower of a slain pop star risks everything to control a form of black magic that will allow him to time travel back and possibly save her life.

"Backstage Pass" was a short story accepted by Seventh Star Press shortly after I'd turned in my draft of *Haunting Obsession*, a Rebecca Burton novella that explores the dangers of fandom from another angle, officially making 2012 "the year R.J. obsessed about obsessive fandom."

Dedicated to the memory of James Townsley (1969-2011), who read through this as a draft and would have loved to see this go "public." I miss you, Jamie. Also dedicated with the greatest love and respect to my hero, C. L. Thornton. Peace and love.

eBay Item: PFLAG Charity Item 2237: Backstage Press Pass—Fiddle Dee-Dee Concert, Astrodome, Houston, Texas, December 21, 1989

Opening Bid: $30—July 12, 2011

Current Bid: $150—July 15, 2011 by <u>Dee Plus</u>

Description: Fiddle Dee-Dee's provocative performance, later referred to as her "coming out party," made her an overnight sensation. The videotape release of the show aired frequently on the cable giant M-TV. Known for her innovative use of 80s pop blended with her classical training as a violinist, Fiddle Dee-Dee shot to the top of the charts with "Women Ride 'Em Sidesaddle" from her debut album *I Don't Give a Dee-Dee*. Just as quickly, the revelation of her same-sex relationship with writing partner Lisa Heathrow—scandalous news at the time—caused her star to plummet.

Dee-Dee donated this backstage pass to the Parents and Friends of Lesbians and Gays (PFLAG) in support of their efforts to create greater awareness for the equality for all persons.

Update July 15: PFLAG was saddened by the tragic death of 80s icon Fiddle Dee-Dee this morning. Though nearly forgotten by today's music fans, the music industry and her small group of loyal followers remember her generosity and spirit always matched her incredible talent.

JARED PRICE LOGGED onto eBay as "Dee Plus" and entered his bid for the backstage pass. He clicked to have further bids texted to his phone. Though a part of him hoped he'd have to bid a couple more times, he knew deep down that $150 was more than enough to secure the pass. Even with her shocking death, Fiddle Dee-Dee no longer grabbed headlines. Only her most devoted fans followed her.

Devoted fans like him.

Jared surfed, surrounded by posters, stacks of yellowed magazines lovingly bagged in Mylar, and a small shelf of autographed CDs—all eight of her official releases and a culling of his favorite rarities and bootleg concerts.

Over time and many get-togethers, Dee graciously signed every one—though she scribbled on the bootlegs rolling her eyes and shaking her head.

Jared logged in to *fiddledeedeemusic.com* and read the memorial message he'd posted as Dee's official webmaster—a position he'd earned from ten years of cultivating Dee's trust and following his idol to show after show.

He read the guest posts, 300 and growing, offering condolences, recalling little kindnesses, or trumpeting Dee's giving nature and gentle personality as much as her talent. He noted the long, personal posts by fellow fans, names he recognized from the newsgroups and fan sites.

Repeating on his DVR for the...he had no idea how many times...he heard the sobbing voice of Lisa Heathrow, Dee-Dee's "widow" in all respects but legally, talking to Piers Morgan of CNN.

A small crowd of heartbroken mourners gathered outside her Broadway apartment. Lisa stood behind the barred gate.

Piers offered his condolences before asking about the attack. "Is it true it happened in front of you?"

Lisa's face drained of color. She drew a deep breath, as if she'd been punched in the gut. "Yes, it's true. I was in the room when ..." Fresh tears sprang into Lisa's eyes, and she lowered her head. "I'm sorry, I thought I could, but...I can't."

The host changed the subject to the legal nightmare Lisa now faced as Dee-Dee's partner for over three decades.

Lisa showed no hesitation. "Dee's brother, as her closest *family*," Lisa spat the word, "sent a lawyer over to impound her bank account and all her property. I sent my own attorney to block his attorney."

Lisa's eyes flashed anger. "Le' me tell you something, Piers. In her will, Dee spells out that I inherit everything. And why not? I co-wrote all of her hit songs. Her *family* had nothing to do with that. I lived in *our* home for almost thirty years, when her *family* wouldn't even speak to her!" Her hands clutched the bars. "But her *family* knows there's money to be claimed, so now we're going to court. Is that fair, Piers?"

Dark circles under Lisa's liquid blue eyes and her unkempt mop of blond hair showed Dee's death had torn her apart, whatever political angle the news wanted to make of it. Lisa, usually soft-spoken and hovering in the background, had always been courteous, even friendly, toward him. He hated what this sudden insanity had done to her.

Jared hated more how his friend and idol was killed by a sick pervert who'd stalked her for years. He'd known him as an obsessed and disturbed freak who had scared the hell out of other fans. Yet, no one had taken action against him.

Ten months earlier—Chicago, October 29, 2010

Jared stood near his friends, Mary Kay, Jamie, Rick, and Michelle, still seated at the table where they'd viewed the track-by-track live performance, essentially loitering in the club after Dee's jazz album release party. While Dee handled the official press back-stage—such as it was—they waited for the coast to clear to hold a private meet n' greet with Dee.

Tony Stoker (dubbed by Dee's fans as "Stoker the Stalker") also waited, his camera with its telescopic lens hanging from one shoulder while he cradled a huge scrapbook against his chest. His gaze darted to their table, around the room, and back again. Tony frequented the newsgroups, so he knew their names. And he knew they had special access.

But they knew *his* name, too. And they knew he *didn't* have special access. At this stage in her career, Dee often showed her few devoted fans incredible consideration, but if she bothered to keep a blacklist, Tony Stoker's name would occupy the top slot.

Jared knew Tony Stoker by name, but not on sight.

As they shook hands, Tony exclaimed, "Oh, you're Jared Price! I'm Tony Stoker. You've been doing her website, right?"

Jared broke eye contact and stared into his drink. *Damn! Now what?* "Dee...Fiddle Dee-Dee...is just one of my clients. I write a syndicated music column. Recently, *Rolling Stone* and *Billboard* invited me to submit some reviews." He braced for Tony's next question.

Tony didn't disappoint. "So...you guys going to meet with her tonight?"

"Nope, definitely not," Jared answered, hoping he didn't sound as much a liar as he suspected.

Tony's arm fell across the back of Jared's shoulders. "Buddy, can I tell you something?"

Jared flinched at the man's piercing, brown-eyed stare—the look of someone who operated on a different plane from the rest of the world.

"I think Dee-Dee is a goddess," he oozed. "Her voice has the power to heal, to hurt, to affect our world. Maybe that's intense, but that's how I feel."

Unfamiliar with how to handle whack jobs, Jared hoped understatement was the proper way to go. "Yeah, uh, that comes off a bit intense."

Stoker the Stalker thrust the scrapbook at him. "I'm a professional photographer, but this book is just my Fiddle Dee-Dee shots."

Opening to a random page, Jared saw eight consecutive photos of Dee on stage, virtually an identical pose, taken rapid-shot. *Why display so many images of the same moment?*

Because he's a whack job. Still, can I really judge another's level of fanaticism? Jared flipped the page.

"Here's one of her coming out of her hotel in Wisconsin last year. I waited in the lobby for six hours." His finger dropped to a photo of Dee, a large canvas hat over her head and dark glasses hiding her eyes. Tony caught her mouth open in a frozen snarl aimed at the cringing blonde next to her. *Lisa.*

Jared knew about the fight, but few others did. He wanted to slug the slimy leech.

The Stalker's voice droned on. "After about four hours, the bellboy asked me if I wanted something to eat. I told him I was fine...."

"Everything okay here?"

His "date," Mary Kay, wandered over from their table. Though Mary Kay was "very gay," they play-dated at concerts. He read the questioning look in her eyes. "Just fine, MK. I was telling Stoker, here," he emphasized the name, "that Dee's calling it an early night."

"Yep!" She ran with the lie. "We were talking about hitting a dance club. Chicago's got a wicked night life, and we wanted to do something positively sinful." She flashed a mischievous smile.

Jared took her hand. "I like how you think. But first, I need to find the restroom." He turned toward Stoker, who looked miserable. "Want to go clubbing?"

"No...I don't think so. Maybe I'll hang out for a few more minutes."

"Suit yourself." He headed for the men's room. Once alone, he pulled out his phone, found the **D. Pat Cell** entry and hit Talk. He kept Fiddle Dee-Dee's name entered under an abbreviation of her lesser-known birth name, Deana Patterson. Last thing he needed was to lose his phone and for someone to find her name and number.

"Hello?" A familiar southern drawl.

"Dee? It's Jared. Sorry to bother you." He always apologized. Fiddle Dee-Dee deserved the proper respect. "We're down here, but a guy named Tony Stoker latched onto us. He's not taking the hint. Tony is——"

"The creepy photo guy?"

"Uh...yeah. Should I tell him we're meeting later?" He heard her sigh.

"Shit, no! I don't need to deal with him tonight. Look, I'm almost done with the reporters. I'll send the bouncer down. He'll pretend to kick everyone out. You wait behind, and after Stalker-man leaves, the bouncer will escort you upstairs. The bouncer's name is Lenny. He knows your name. I told him he can trust you to point out who's in our group."

She trusts me. A childish flush flowed over him. "Sounds good."

The ploy worked. Tony the Stalker wandered away, Jared's group doubled back, and they hung out in Dee-Dee's dressing room, getting advance autographed copies of *Summertime*, posing for photos, and drinking cheap wine until sunup.

JARED NEVER SAW TONY AGAIN, but their bizarre meeting replayed every time CNN flashed the mugshot of "Stoker the Stalker."

Jared recalled his anger at the scrapbook and seeing Dee's hurt captured on film. The couple had quarreled over whether to continue co-writing original material or follow the demands of the record label—standards—relegating Dee to the nightclub circuit. Jared first heard about it when Dee called him to "get your ass over here" to discuss the marketing.

---

14 MONTHS EARLIER, June 22, 2010

Jared rushed over to Dee and Lisa's apartment to discuss the new direction. They gathered in the couple's modest dining room, promotional proofs spread out before them. Before long, Dee and Lisa told him about their disagreement. But, in the telling, the fight started again. Their voices rose, tones sharpened.

Without warning, Lisa stood, slapping her palms on the tabletop and scattering papers. She leaned close to Jared. "You know what she said to me?"

The sour wine on her breath made Jared cringe.

Lisa continued, "Dee said, 'I'll always love you, but I don't trust you to write my music anymore.' What am I supposed to *say* to that shit?"

Lisa darted from his sight. He heard her footfalls as she left the room and ran down the hall. The slamming door made Jared flinch. He looked away, trying to project the appropriate shock at the unfolding drama. Eyes downcast, he snuck a peek at his idol, sitting across from him, shaking her head.

"I didn't mean it like that!" Dee yelled, apparently knowing the exact volume to penetrate the door.

Jared gathered his papers. "I should go."

Dee gripped his forearm. "No, it's okay, sweetie."

As much as wished he couuld deny it, he wanted to do a quiet "fist pump" in the air. He'd just witnessed a moment of private pain between two people. And his first response? Giddy joy. Because he was a fan who held status with his idol. How pathetic am I? Ashamed, he pushed the emotion down deep, so far down that he might even be able to lie to himself later. He dropped his folders on the table and placed his hand over hers, patting it a bit longer than necessary. "It's going to be okay. She'll come around."

Dee nodded. "I know. I'm just in the doghouse for a few days." She pulled her hands back and wiped her palms across her face. "Okay, focus. The album is called *Summertime*, and we're releasing it in October, because that makes perfect sense to the record company. The photo shoot is tomorrow. I'll email the pings to you...."

JARED ADDED a link to the Piers Morgan interview onto *fiddledeedeemusic.com* and Dee's Facebook and Twitter. Once again, he stared at the tear-streaked eyes of his idol's soulmate.

Jared released a drawn-out sigh. Their apartment was a twenty-minute walk from his own, and he felt an urge to see her.

He grabbed his iPod. Usually, when he couldn't deal with the world, Dee-Dee's soothing voice calmed his shattered nerves, but he didn't think he could handle hearing her voice. He settled for Sarah McLachlan. Minutes later, Jared rang the buzzer on box 304, "Dee and Lisa" scrawled in black Sharpie. A staticky voice greeted him.

"H'lo?"

"Hi...Lisa. It's Jared. The website guy." He glanced over at a group of mourners, maybe a dozen, huddled together in vigil.

"Come in."

He heard the buzz, gave the gate a shove, and entered the plain, low-lit hallway. After a quick elevator ride to the third floor, he stood outside her door. Dee and Lisa never moved out of the working-class apartment where they'd written their original, breakthrough songs. He knocked on the solid oak door. At the muffled call of "come in," he entered.

Lisa sat, shriveled in the corner of the oversized couch, hugging her knees, tears flowing down her face.

He glanced at her, then looked away and began babbling to the wall. "I don't know...I just felt like I should be here. Now it feels like a mistake, but I wanted——"

"I heard the table shatter and ran out of the bedroom."

What? He looked up, meeting her eyes and looked at her——really *looked* at her——for the first time.

Lisa nodded, the look on her face confirming what she didn't dare say aloud. *You heard me right.* She indicated the floor in front of them.

Jared stared at the open iron framework that once held a glass tabletop. Lisa's voice reached him from across a void.

"He was straddling her. And there was glass and blood everywhere. He ..."

The power of the vicarious vision her words formed in his mind forced the air from his lungs. He fell back against the wall, sliding down onto the floor. He saw in vivid clarity, Dee splayed on the floor, Stoker crouched over her chest, yelling into her face.

Lisa continued the story, but Jared heard the screams in Tony's voice.

"He yelled, 'I said one more picture, Dee! I'm not leaving until I get it!' And he raised his camera and pounded it down. I don't think she was awake to feel it. Oh, God. And I heard the crunch and I...I didn't help her! It was too late, and God help me, I didn't want to die. I ran to the bedroom, locked the door, and called 911."

The reports never said what happened. But now Jared knew (*because I'm* special, *lucky me!*) Dee died because she tried to extend kindness to a fan, like so many times before. The talented, beautiful woman with the soothing voice had been permanently silenced because her trusting nature had finally worked against her.

He wanted to cry, but a clamp in his gut locked down tight. He took a shuddering breath and approached the couch. In desperation, he extended his arms.

Lisa fell into them. "What am I going to do?" she wailed. "Oh, God, she's gone. What am I going to do now?"

"It's okay, it's all right." He stroked her rough, over-bleached blond hair, staring at the wall and trying to ignore the damp of tears and mucus gathering on his chest.

After a good long cry, her breathing calmed, and her head slumped.

She'd fallen asleep. He waited many minutes, trying to ignore the cramp in his back and arms.

Lisa stirred and lifted her head. "Oh. I'm sorry." She separated herself from him, looking down to the floor. "Thank you. Look, I have to do some things, but I want you to have something." She vanished to the bedroom and returned with a box.

Jared turned up the cardboard flap. The items inside left him speechless. Stacks of 45 singles stamped "Promo," acetate originals, marketing packets, and programs. As he rummaged through the box, he saw a distinct black scribble on most of them—the heart and xx kiss autograph scrawl he knew on sight, followed by a giant "D."

"These are...they…" He couldn't speak. *Why am I getting these?*

"Dee signed these; she cleaned out her attic of this old shit and was going to donate them to PFLAG. I don't even know how to reach them—pathetic, right?"

"I won the backstage pass that went up last week," Jared added.

"Well, this is the kind of stuff Dee's brother is looking for, anything left behind worth decent cash now that she's...gone. I'll be *damned* if he's going to get them. Oh, and here." Lisa grabbed three boxy paperweights from the side table and dropped them into the box.

Her Grammy awards? "Lisa, I can't...."

"Yes, you can. Now go. Give them to the fans. Tell them she loved them." She shooed him out.

He cradled the cardboard box against his chest, walking like a robot. If the small gathering of fans knew what he carried, they'd strip him of his treasures in seconds, but he continued the several blocks to his modest apartment unmolested.

He stopped before four silhouettes on the front steps of his apartment. Standing in near-darkness, he swallowed back panic. *Someone from the vigil figured it out.*

Then he recognized the crooked smile of his friend Mary Kay, flanked by Michelle, Rick, and Jamie. He grinned as he placed the cardboard box on the ground to receive their group embrace.

Mary Kay lived in Key West, Jamie from Canada, and Rick from Chicago. Michelle was his only other local New York "Dee-Buddy." Their arms folded around him.

Her head cradled against his chest, Mary spoke. "We felt we should all be together now."

Delighted, he led them into his apartment, and gathered them around while he presented the box.

"No way!" Jamie held up the Grammy statuette.

They surrounded the box, fondling various pieces, speechless.

"What are we going to do with this?" Michelle asked.

Jared carefully lowered a 45 sleeve back down into the box. "I've been thinking—Lisa's legal fees are going to be crazy. We can put this stuff on eBay to help her. It might not fetch a lot, but enough to let her quietly move out and start again."

Minutes later, Jared slid the Houston concert Blu-Ray into his player. He cued up the show and let his mind go blank for the first time since hearing the news.

"Houston, do you give a damn?" she screeched from the tiny TV speakers.

As the opening chords blared, the first stirrings of emotion welled up inside him.

Mary Kay and Michelle sniffled and dabbed their eyes with tissues.

Several minutes into the video, Jared wiped his hands across his cheeks, finally releasing the pain and anger bottled up inside.

For the next ninety minutes, the room filled with a rocking, siren-ous voice mingled with open weeping.

THE NEXT MORNING, the backstage pass arrived in the mail, and the beginnings of a plan formed in Jared's mind.

JARED WAITED, drumming his fingers against the bare wood table top while staring at the empty chair across from him. He didn't want this appointment. He'd fought against scheduling one. But yesterday, when he'd spoken with Agent Burke...no, her name was Burton...she'd insisted that her information on Avalon Incorporated was too sensitive to be given out over the phone, or even emailed. They'd have to meet face to face. "That seems awfully inefficient, even for a government agency," he'd said into the receiver.

"Your tax dollars at work," Burton had quipped. "Please don't do anything until we meet. I can be there tomorrow."

So now, a day later, he sat in a small meeting room within New York City Hall, reserved for some government sub-branch called the Special Investigations Unit, waiting. He couldn't help but notice how the bare room, with only a narrow table and a chair on each side, could serve for an interrogation just as easily as a consultation.

It had taken Jared almost a year to track down Avalon Incorporated, a dummy, small business set up as a gateway for people searching for individuals with "special talents." These talents ranged from serving as psychic mediums and fortune tellers to even more outlandish claims, if he could believe the stories.

Curiosity got the better of him. Mostly, he just wanted to know the reputation of Avalon Incorporated before he handed over his money to them, so he started at ground zero—he called the local Chamber of Commerce. The chamber director picked up, and upon Jared mentioning Avalon Incorporated, he had to promise not to hang up the phone, and then found himself put on hold. Several minutes later, the director had transferred his call to Agent Burton of Special Investigations, who insisted on the face-to-face.

At first, Jared thought the whole thing was some elaborate joke, with the entire scenario unfolding like a scene from a cheap thriller. A part of this nonsense alarmed him, but Jared kept assuring himself he'd done nothing wrong. He was just asking questions.

The door opened, and a woman entered, dressed in a stylish black leather jacket over a business casual blouse and black slacks. She wore a dark fedora atop her head. She nodded and took the seat across from him, extending her hand.

"Mister Price, I'm Rebecca Burton, Special Investigations. Thank you for meeting with me today."

He reached out to shake hands.

She took his and pumped her arm in a single shake.

He started to let go, but she retained her grip, keeping their hands clasped across the table.

"I hope I didn't alarm you, but when you inquired about Avalon, we wanted to share some important information...."

A sudden wave of vertigo struck him, and her voice diminished, sounding like it came from a great distance. As she continued to hold his hand, something tingled, like electricity, from her palm.

"...the nature of your business?"

Jared pulled his hand away. "I'm sorry, what?"

"I asked if you could share the nature of your business with Avalon."

Hell no. Jared shook his head to clear it. "That's confidential. Look, my inquiry was pretty straightforward. I know the word on the streets. They do...extraordinary things, if half the rumors are true. I just want to know, are they true to their word?"

Burton removed the hat and placed it on the table between them. She gave her head a fast shake, and her bright red hair dropped down to frame her pale face. She regarded him with striking green eyes. "That's not an easy question to answer, Mister Price. What I can tell you is that Sparkle is a woman of her word."

"Sparkle?"

"Avalon Incorporated, in spite of the implication of the name, is really a one-person operation. She goes by the name Sparkle. We have no other aliases on her."

"That sounds ..." He didn't want to be rude, but he could think of no other word, "...ludicrous."

Burton shrugged. "Perhaps. Nevertheless, Sparkle is not a fake, a charlatan, or a con artist. She can do exactly what she says she can do and will stick to the letter of any agreement she enters into with you."

Jared released a breath. *Great. That's all I needed to know.* He started to rise from his chair.

Burton's next words stopped him in mid-motion. "And that is why I hope to discourage you from even speaking with her."

He dropped back down into the seat. "I don't understand. I thought you said she can really do what she claims."

"Mr. Price, one of the purposes of the Special Investigations Unit is to confirm all claims of an extraordinary or paranormal nature. Most people don't know that New York has a department of this sort, because most people need to be driven into a dire circumstance before they even seek out our services. It would really help if you could share with me how you hope Avalon Incorporated could help you."

Jared shrugged. "I'm sorry. I don't see how that matters. No offense, but I've already scheduled a consultation with Avalon Incorporated for tomorrow. Nothing I've heard here makes me think I need to cancel that appointment." More determined than ever, he rose and stepped toward the door.

"I loved her music, too."

Burton's voice stopped him in his tracks. He turned. *Did I hear her right?* "Excuse me?"

Burton shook her head. As she spoke, she stared down at the floor. "When I was a little girl, 'Women Ride 'Em Sidesaddle' was my favorite song. I remember my father playing the song over and over on his CD player in the living room, for minutes at a time. I used to dance...well, twirl, really...as the song played through the house." A nostalgic smile matched the faraway look in her eyes.

"How did you know I was——?"

Burton's gaze rose to meet his. "What happened to Fiddle Dee-Dee was a terrible tragedy. I don't mean to belittle you or minimize your pain. It's horrible every time a good person dies for a bad reason. Sooner or later, if we live long enough, we see more than our share of unfair and unnecessary suffering. Sometimes we're the victims of it. But it's a part of living, something we have to accept about the real world...until the time comes when we must face our own death."

Jared's body shook at the impact of her words. "I should have done something. I should have recognized the signs."

Burton shook her head. "She was a lucky woman to have such devoted friends."

Jared was grateful Burton didn't use the word "fans."

Burton continued, "She was also lucky because of what she left behind." She stepped around the table.

Before he could respond, she reached out and grabbed his hand again.

"Jared, I can play her music any time I want to. All I have to do is listen, and I can *be* that joyful little girl again and relive those wonderful memories. That's the legacy she's left us. That's what she's left *all* of us. She and other singers just like her. It's a *good* legacy, Jared. Be satisfied with that."

A strange sensation traveled up his hand and into his body. Calm settled over him. *Maybe I should just listen.*

But he couldn't. "No!" He yanked his hand out of hers with sudden force. "Listen. Clearly you have some powers of your own. The way I see it, there's no reason not to keep my appointment with Avalon Incorporated, and at least hear this Sparkle person out." More determined than ever, he stepped away from her. "Besides, if I get into trouble, you can always come find me and bail me out."

Rebecca shook her head. "I wouldn't count on that."

"Why not?"

"Because, depending on what you agree to, you might end up beyond my help. Sparkle's powers are such that she can send you beyond *anyone's* help."

Jared drew a shaky breath. "That's a chance I'll have to take." Without another word, he turned and left Rebecca Burton standing alone in the room.

THE NEXT DAY, Jared kept his appointment. Five minutes into the meeting, shifting in the second-hand loveseat, he started to second-guess the wisdom of doing so.

Sparkle smiled, exposing gaps in her crooked teeth. "What makes you think I can help you?"

Sparkle, a heavyset, trailer-trash, bleached blonde, sat in the brown leather chair across from him. As best Jared could tell, she was age twenty or fifty or anywhere in between.

Votive candles, scattered across a zebra-striped rug and clustered on small tables against the walls, offered the only light in a tiny room assigned a suite number under "Avalon Incorporated." The candles created a glowing frame in the claustrophobic cubby.

"I said, 'What makes you think I can help you?'"

The edge in Sparkle's voice brought Jared back to the discussion. "I don't know that you can. I only know that, if it can be done, it can't be accomplished through technology. So I'm forced to pursue...less conventional methods."

The woman nodded with dramatic flair. She wore a black, hooded cloak pulled back on her shoulders. *Problematic clothing, given the exposed candles all over the room.* Each of her chubby fingers held an oversized ring, and the countless bangles around her wrists jingled with each move of her arms. Jared scoffed to himself. *Agent Burton says this woman is not a charlatan?*

Sparkle sat with elbows bent and hands folded before her like a queen. "You mean, magic. The dark arts, powers which druids like me manipulate to the disbelief of the outside world." The theatrics dropped from her voice. "You remember that snowfall in Arizona last year? That was one of mine."

Jared sighed. "Really?"

Sparkle nodded. "Bon Jovi's last hit single. That was me, too."

Jared considered. "Actually, that makes a lot of sense. But those accomplishments seem minor compared to…" He added his own flair. *Why not?* "…changing the past. Time travel."

"Changing the past is simply about giving people the opportunity to approach the same moment so they can make a different choice." She leaned forward and placed a meaty hand on his lap, squeezing his upper thigh.

Jared tried not to react in any way that might offend her.

"You're approaching your own choice. One is where we work

together. The other is where you walk out that door, and we never see each other again." She removed her hand.

Jared released a breath he hadn't realized he was holding.

She wiggled two fingers before his face, rings clicking together. "Two choices, two dimensions formed, but only one choice becomes 'our' reality." Sparkle rose from her chair, her rustling black robe barely concealing the curvy contours of her overdeveloped form. "The real problem is finding a way to break your physical body out of *this* reality, and break you back in where you can affect the past to create a different future from the one in place now."

Jared rubbed his temples. She was giving him a headache. "Okay, so we redefine the problem as you said it. Can you do it?"

"Yes."

"And how do I know that?"

Sparkle smiled. "Do you remember the nuclear accident in 1997 that destroyed most of California?"

"What are you talking about? Of course not."

"Exactly." She giggled. "That was one of mine, too."

"Oh, *very* cute."

"But nevertheless true."

"Really? Then what about what happened in Japan last year? Or were you hibernating for the winter when that one hit?"

Sparkle's eyes flashed anger, but her smile never left. "I'm a mercenary. If someone wanted to undo the Japan event and had the resources, I would have helped."

Jared pounded a fist into the arm of the loveseat. "Dammit, I'll give everything to fix this. But I can't pay handsomely."

"Nor do you have to." Her hand returned to his thigh, pressing urgently.

The action didn't bother him as much. And he found her voice soothing.

"Time is far more flexible than some fanciful sci-fi authors would have you think." Sparkle stroked her hand up and down his lap. Her eyes glazed over

He no longer felt the urge to fidget, but he shook off sudden lethargy. "What are you saying?"

Sparkle refocused. "I'm saying that whether your precious pop star lives or dies makes almost no difference. Does it matter which flash-in-the-pan pop idol plays Madison Square Garden next month?" Again, she withdrew her hand. "Who does it affect beyond the fanatic followers? To most people, it's a one-night distraction."

"Fuck you, too." Jared smiled. "And thank you very much. You're not at all like Rebecca said you were."

"Rebecca Burton?" Sparkle shrugged. "I'm sure she said terrible things about me. She's a woman of incredible potential, but she's afraid of her own power. I am not." She reached into her robe and produced a folded paper. "Here are the terms of our contract, including the bottom line." She spread the oddly modern-looking computer-printed contract open and pointed with a pen at the monetary figure toward the bottom.

"Wow, that's...going to take a while to raise."

Sparkle giggled.

The sound pleased him. Moment by moment, the woman across from him grew more attractive. The curves beneath her robe tightened and firmed. He pulled his gaze from her young, attractive face. A thought occurred to him, which forced a laugh. "You—" He pointed with a hand he could barely raise. "You wouldn't drug me, right?"

She flashed a glamorous smile at him, luscious lips pulled back to reveal perfect teeth. "Sign here, please."

Jared scribbled his initials.

Her robe dropped to the floor, revealing tight, rounded breasts above a flat stomach. She uncrossed her athletic legs, as if to purposefully let him contemplate the promises of the flesh between her thighs.

"What's—?"

She leaned forward, mouth open.

He tasted cinnamon in her kiss.

"The magic requires the bonding of our bodies and our spirits. I took some steps to make us more comfortable with this part of the transaction. I didn't think you'd mind."

Jared didn't mind at all.

A PHONE CONVERSATION, 2012

Jared: Hey, Chaz, how've you been?

Chaz: Jared? Wow, man, it's been forever. Is that any way to treat your lifelong best friend?

Jared: Sorry, I've been...terribly busy. How's the new video game project coming?

Chaz: Behind schedule, as usual. How's the writing? I saw the Dee tribute in *Rolling Stone*. Nice stuff.

Jared: Thanks. I promised her I'd get her back on the cover someday. Of course, I didn't...well, it was from the heart. So, listen. Let's get together and down a few. You know, catch up.

Chaz: It's been too long, buddy. Anything wrong?

Jared: I don't know. I might be taking a trip soon, and I'm not sure when I'm coming back.

JARED PRICE OPENED his eyes in 1989.

A few minutes ago (or would that be 23 years later?), Jared

dropped an envelope through a mail slot. The envelope was addressed to Rebecca Burton, care of the Special Investigations Unit, New York City Building, and contained a letter explaining his intentions and his plans, in the hopes that, if something went wrong, perhaps the investigator would find some way to help him.

The letter mailed, he walked into a Holiday Inn in Houston, Texas. He bypassed the front desk as if heading to a room and stopped in a hallway. He squeezed his eyes shut, poured the small vial of green powder onto his tongue, and swallowed rapidly.

According to his research, the Inn was first constructed in 1974, making it a stable structure for time traveling. It was also a ten-minute taxi ride to the Astrodome.

When he opened his eyes, the wall paint changed color, and the air held a thicker, dirtier quality. He shook off dizziness and pivoted toward the lobby——only to dodge a heavy ,cylindrical cement obstacle at hip-level——a freestanding ashtray, filled with butts. Looking around, he saw several other stubs strewn on the floor.

He stifled a giggle. *How could I forget? I'm twenty years away from enforced anti-smoking laws.* He left several items back in the year 2012 because they would be useless or conspicuous——credit cards, cell phone, laptop——even his iPod, which he took everywhere. Over the last few months, he'd gathered a decent collection of older cash in various denominations.

He wore a basic, striped polo shirt, a pair of Levi's blue jeans, classic canvas Converse tennis shoes, and a jean jacket. The collar looked too small by 80s styles, and the jeans fit tight at the ankles. It would have to do.

— — —

SINCE 1997, Jared had attended sixteen Fiddle Dee-Dee shows. From a couple of six- to eight-thousand seat amphitheaters to many more sold out intimate shows of five hundred or fewer seats. Even in such small settings, Dee could still excite a crowd into a frenzy of screaming crazies.

Somewhere in the small town of Perionne, Indiana, he imagined his tenth-grade self struggling with the tuner of his cassette boombox to find the problematic radio signal broadcasting Fiddle Dee-Dee history. And here he stood, with no practical way to tell his teenage self that, through some literal miracle, he'd returned as a thirty-something fan to relive this pinnacle moment in his idol's career.

Only 15 years old in 1989, he never caught a Fiddle Dee-Dee show until her relevance had diminished by almost a decade of public indifference. So he'd never seen...this.

Crazy punk hair. The wild colors. The smell of bodies pushing toward the stage. The *noise.* The cries of adoration from an arena full of raving fans, **Dee! Dee! Dee! Dee!** Coalescing into a single call of ecstasy as the houselights dimmed. A single spotlight illuminated the tiny singer with the ripped, sleeveless top and rainbow Mohawk, cradling a violin under her chin, running her bow across an intentional discord to draw the audience's attention.

"DEEEEEEEEEEEEEEEEEEE!!!"

"HOUSTON, TEXAS, DO YOU GIVE A DAMN!"

Dee called out in exact synch with the angry tone preserved on his DVD back home. But his recording failed to capture the sheer decibel level of the crowd's exuberance.

He knew every song, every side comment to the audience, and every action. But he understood it—*lived* it—for the first time. The next two hours passed in a blur as Jared finally witnessed the Dee he knew was buried deep inside.

IN THE AFTERGLOW, Jared forgot *why* he was there.

He turned toward the exit, intending to hop on the internet and tell his friends he'd just seen the *best damn* Fiddle Dee-Dee show *ever!*

Then he remembered. He was lost in the past to create a better future for him, for his friends, and for Dee. But first...

Minutes later, he emerged from the restroom, having dressed in a souvenir T-shirt and clasping a program. He'd tossed the polo in the trash, telling himself the look would give him away. But that was an excuse. He just wanted to buy the T-shirt. The ultimate souvenir to the ultimate joyride.

He weaved his way through the thinning crowd to a security guard—*they wore obnoxious yellow jackets back then, too*—and presented his press pass.

After a moment of intense scrutiny, the burly guard pointed to a door to the left of the stage. "Show it there. Ask for Ricky."

Jared nodded, comfortable with the "meet 'n greet" process to get backstage to so many of Dee's past shows. *Future shows.* The only difference, of course, was that Dee didn't know him. *Yet.*

The crowd culled to a few clusters—mainly fanatics, while some waited out the traffic jam. Still others meeting to hit the local bars.

Jared skirted his way to the side stage door. He handed his press pass to the security man. "I was told to ask for Ricky."

"You got him."

This guard, just as burly as the other, but with salt-colored specks in his dark hair, also examined Jared's badge. For several seconds.

For more than several seconds.

Just as Jared opened his mouth to offer a lame explanation about the pass, the guard handed it back.

"Okay, who you with?"

"*Chronicle.* Need a few quotes as a sidebar to the review tomorrow."

"Uh-huh. Shouldn't you have gotten those at the press conference?"

Jared grinned, hoping he showed his best "hungry journalist" face. "Can't blame a guy for wanting an exclusive with one of the hottest singers of the year."

Ricky shook his head. "Uh-huh. I'll see if she can spare ya five minutes. She's already meeting with her fan club and that can take a while. I don't suppose you can guarantee a good review?"

Jared laughed. "I don't know how it can go any other way."

"Uh-huh. Follow me." Ricky pushed his way through the door.

Jared stepped after him, plunging into near-darkness, following the man down a long hallway.

They passed a closed door with an emergency bar. Squeals of teenybopper rapture escaped into the hallway. "Everything you play is *totally* amazing!" Another chorus of high-pitched screams.

Jared heard the measured, flattered tone of Dee's response, though not her actual words.

Ricky opened the door to a large dressing/locker room.

Old beer and other unsavory odors assaulted him, a reminder he'd returned to the decadent 80s, where rock stars fairly earned their reputation for accepting whatever gracious gifts their groupies cared to offer.

"Okay, pal. I'll let her know you're here and...we'll see."

"Thanks very much."

The dressing room reminded him of his high school gym locker room, with a cement floor and a long wooden bench, bolted down and running along the front of perhaps a dozen lockers. Spacious enough to house an entire band, Jared noted only one large trunk set down in the corner—a chest-high black box with bright, neon pink tape across the front, the letter "D" scrawled in black marker.

Along the opposite wall, Jared spied a hand dryer and a row of sinks, and, around the corner, a set of urinals and toilets. Knowing he probably had several minutes, Jared answered nature's call. Upon his return, the first case of real nerves hit, and he dropped down onto the stiff, bolted-down, backless bench.

He'd fought and lied and maneuvered his way here. *Now what?* Though he'd taken this trip to save Dee from a terrible death, he realized his ambitions went beyond that. He could change her career now. He had knowledge she needed to avoid years of languishing obscurity, and extend her wave of success for years, maybe decades, if he could convince her not to make the mistake that wrecked her momentum so early.

Jared stood and started walking back and forth. Pacing wasn't something he normally did, but the nervous energy coursing through his body demanded some sort of action. He reached into his pocket and gripped the vial of powder that would return him to the present. A present, he hoped, where Dee had earned superstar status, to Amazon listings of multiple greatest hits volumes, to a chain of bestselling releases completely unfamiliar to him. After all, it was her indie-star desperation that led Dee to abandon pop material and explore her talents as a songwriter.

And I love that material. Much of it proved better than her pop hits. Melancholy flowed over him. He'd heard music that might no longer exist in this new reality.

In this future, the odds were, she wouldn't know him. Superstars such as Elvis Presley or Michael Jackson turned recluse, experts at avoiding the legions of crazies. He could only watch from a distance with millions of other admirers.

This is the last gift I can give her.

The door opened, and Jared stopped mid-step, gawking in spite of himself. The amused glow in her eyes, the familiar arching eyebrows, the cheerful grin. She stood before him younger and far more attractive than he'd ever seen her in person, but what surprised him most was her confident stance, the authority with which she extended her arm for a handshake, her rainbow-streaked hair standing in its iconic Mohawk he'd only before seen in old photos and posters.

"Dee!"

Her hand gripped his in a firm grasp, then pulled away before he could place his hand over hers.

"Dee? My, aren't we familiar?" Jared felt his face flame, but her friendly smile reassured him. "It's okay, I'm just surprised you got it right. Most reporters say, 'Ms. Dee-Dee', or they might call me 'Fiddle,' for Christ's sakes."

Jared laughed. Like the first few times he'd met her, he floundered, star-struck and fighting an adrenaline rush that made it difficult to speak.

She waited for him to find his voice

"Sorry, Dee, I didn't mean to catch you off guard. You can call me Jared, and we'll be even."

"Fair enough, Jared."

"And...there's something else."

Dee cocked her head, a strained look behind her glimmering gaze.

Jared decided to go for the truth—at least, part of it. "I'm sorry, Dee. See, I'm a big fan. I've written for *Rolling Stone* and *Billboard*, and I almost never get flustered in the presence of celebrities. But...well, frankly, I think you're awesome."

"Awww. How sweet!" Her grin widened, and she extended her hand again, this time allowing him to place his over hers. "You have bylines in *Rolling Stone*? Jared...what's your last name?"

Uh-oh! "Price."

"Jared Price? I don't recall that name."

"Well ..." Again, he stuck close to the truth. "I mainly write reviews and edit copy of feature writers' articles. I haven't really had many bylines. Tiny things." Jared chuckled. "Slowly working my way up." *Very slowly. My first byline won't appear for another twenty years.*

"Uh huh." Her smile faded, replaced by...doubt? Anger? "Mister Price, exactly what can I do for you?"

"Well, I was hoping to supplement tomorrow's review with some sidebar quotes—"

"Right, for the local paper. So Ricky explained. Editing bylines for *Rolling Stone, Billboard,* and now some sidebar quotes for someone else's review. Looks like you're writing for a lot of places, but no one's heard of you."

Words exploded from him. "Okay, you're right. I have an ulterior motive for seeing you."

She laughed and patted his arm. "I know, you're a fan, and I'm flattered. And I'll pose for a picture before you go. But ..." She stopped. Her brow furrowed. "You *are* doing the article you said you are...right?"

Jared opened his mouth to lie, but the words stuck in his throat. Instead, the truth came out. "No...no, I'm not. I'm here to warn you. To try and help you, but you're going to have a hard time understanding or believing me."

Dee's back stiffened. This time anger—no doubt about it—flashed in her eyes. "Mister, if you're not with the press, you have no damn business being in my dressing room."

"Dee, please, listen to me—" He stepped toward her but her hand shot out and pressed against his chest as a firm warning.

"No, *you* listen. Just this morning, a man jumped up on stage during sound check, got down on his knees, and proposed marriage. Then he came at me with handcuffs! So if you're some sort of freak who thinks we have some special connection because my song spoke to you, I don't have the patience today."

He closed his eyes, finding it hard to breathe. The meeting was falling apart. *I have to grab her attention!* "Dee, I know about you and Lisa."

"Lisa! Listen, Mister Familiarity. I never claimed to write all my songs. Her co-writing credits are on the liner notes."

"No, Dee, I *know* about you and Lisa! I know that you're lovers!"

Dee glared at him. The moment dragged out. "We don't exactly keep it a secret from our friends, pal! If you're looking for some sort of hush money, you'd better—"

"No, no, please listen, I'm not after anything. I'm trying to help you. I know you and Lisa are planning to 'out' yourselves in *Rolling Stone* next month."

"'Out' ourselves? What the hell does—"

"Sorry. You're planning to go public about your relationship."

"Well...yeah, in fact, we talked about it just last night...for the first time." Again, she glared. "But how the hell would you know that? We haven't mentioned it to anyone."

"That's not all I know, Dee. Please, listen. If I don't stop you, the announcement will hit about a month and a half from now. And—" He snapped his fingers. "—that will be the end of your career—at least, this superstar era of your career—before it ever takes off."

"Bullshit! Tell that to Elton John. He admitted to being bisexual years ago, and he's doing just fine."

"He's not bi, he's gay." *Oh, crap, I did it again.* "But never mind. Elton had years of hits before he even revealed that much."

"Oh, so it's okay for *him*, but *I* have to go on living a lie?"

"No, Dee, of *course* it's not all right. It's never all right, and one day...not long from now...public opinion will change. But I can tell you...I promise you! If you go forward with that interview, you'll regret it. Listen, I'm not saying that you'll stop recording. But you'll lose the masses, and you'll never get them back. And deep down, at your most vulnerable, you'll admit it was a mistake. You'll admit it to Lisa and to...to your friends. You'll wish you waited, just a few years longer."

"Okay, so you came to give me career advice. You looked into your crystal ball, and it said not to do the *Rolling Stone* interview. Okay, Jared, thanks very much."

"Dee, don't condescend to me. I hate it when you do that."

"Who the *fuck* are you to talk to me like that? You come in here under false pretenses and act like we're old friends?"

Jared reached out to grab her.

Instead, she thrust a small fist at his chest, the impact sharp, stinging. "I don't owe you shit, and I know *damn* well I've never seen you before." She turned.

"Wait!" He gasped through excruciating pain, blinking through a sheen of tears. He saw rings of metal across the knuckles of the hand that clipped him.

"Ricky!" she yelled.

"No, Dee, wait." He reached out, grabbing her shoulder.

She spun in mid-step, placing both her hands firmly against his chest. She snarled. "I'm not interested in anything you have to say!"

He screamed back, his words overpowering hers. "You're going to die if I don't warn you!" He grabbed both of her shoulders.

"Are you threatening me?"

"No! I want to help you. Twenty four years from now, you'll die at the hands of a stalker if you don't listen to me. I know. I was there!"

"What!" Her eyes widened—discs of disbelief.

"I'm from the future, Dee. I'm your friend in 2011, and you died. And I couldn't stop it, so I went back in time to stop it. That's the whole truth."

"You *are* crazy!"

"I knew you wouldn't believe me, but I can help you. I know what happens. I traveled back in time to help you because I love you. You have to believe me."

She sprang away and cut the air with a shrill scream.

"Fucking freak! Leave me alone! Ricky!"

"No!"

She bolted full-speed toward the door.

Jared jumped after her, not sure how to stop her from shouting again. He fell toward the floor but reached out toward her retreating leg.

"Ricky, help! Lisa!"

His fingers grasped her ankle. As his body hit the floor, he pulled roughly on her ankle, tripping her. Honest to God, he let go as soon as he realized.

Dee fell. Hard. Toward the long wooden bench.

A crack echoed through the chamber, the horrible sound of a skull breaking against a wooden plane, reinforced with metal and bolted to cement.

Sprawled on the floor, Jared could only watch, adding his cry of anguish where hers cut off.

Her petite body rolled off the bench and slumped to the ground, eyes already lifeless.

A pool of blood formed a ghastly silhouette around her head.

The door flew open with a loud bang. The noise brought Jared to his senses. He could return, go forward, where he came from, maybe try again...

He thrust his hand into his denim pocket. The vial lay under him.

He heard shouts and yells of confusion. He tried to ignore them as he struggled.

He pivoted onto his side, finally pinching the precious vial, pulling the glass free.

He reached toward his mouth just as a tremendous weight pounced on his back, pummeling him to the cement, causing the vial to fly from his fingers and shatter on the floor.

"No! I can fix this, I can——!"

Fingers dug into his neck, shoving his face into the ground once, twice, he lost count and could only lie on the ground, dazed, hearing the pandemonium.

"You sick son of a bitch!"

"Look, drugs! Get it!"

"Is she——"

He made one final effort, but bodies pinned him to the floor.

Through the heavy breathing, the pulling and scuffling, a piercing scream penetrated the pile of bodies. *Lisa.*

A cry tore from Lisa's throat, twenty four years premature. "Oh, baby, baby, no! You can't be!"

As rough hands pulled and buffeted him, Jared descended into blackness.

A PHONE CONVERSATION, Perionne, Indiana, December 22, 1989

Chaz: Damn, Jared. I don't know what to say. It's...it's just terrible.

Jared: I listened to her show on the radio last night, and this morning she's dead! And the sick bastard has the same name as me!

Chaz: Have you seen him? He *looks* like you!

Jared: What? Fuck off! He does not. Like I don't feel weird enough.

Chaz: Sorry. M-TV had detectives on who said the back-stage pass was brilliant. But the psycho won't say anything.

Jared: Well...what can he say? What a fucking waste. Fiddle Dee-Dee was so talented, she could have done so much, if only she'd been given a chance....

JARED STRUGGLED AGAINST A DARK FUNK.

Locked in a tiny room, Jared's drug-befuddled mind (for they kept him on heavy sedatives) took several days to realize the full consequence of what he'd done. He'd killed her. He'd tried to save her, and he'd destroyed her instead.

At first, a name burned on his mind, a bright spot of hope in his world of darkness. *Special Agent Rebecca Burton.*

He'd sent her the letter, explained what he'd hoped to do. In the future, twenty four years from now, if he held out that long, she'd come to help him. He'd even convinced himself she could find a way to follow him. All he'd have to do was cling to sanity long enough for her to find him.

Long days slipped into long weeks, which slipped into long months. His mind cleared from the shock, and he adjusted to a new sense of normal. He endured the beatings and other nastiness from the orderlies, the result that always followed their horrified reaction whenever they learned who he was. They knew how to beat people in ways that didn't show the bruises. He couldn't even hate them for what they did. After all, he'd do the same thing if the roles were reversed.

No one would come for him. He knew that now. No one *could* come for him. With increased clarity came increased understanding. He remembered Rebecca's final warning to him. "You might be beyond my help. Her powers are such that she can send you beyond *anyone's* help."

He added Rebecca's warning to Sparkle's explanation and definition of time travel. "The real problem is finding a way to break your physical body out of *this* reality, and break you back in, *where you can affect the past to create a different future from the one in place now.*"

He'd certainly affected the past and created a different future. In this different future, Dee would never die at the hands of a stalker in the year 2011. In this different future, there would be no bereaved Jared to send a note of explanation to a future Inspector Burton. If Burton received that letter, she was cut off from him, in another dimension, still in the original timeline from which he'd separated himself. Beyond her help. Just another client of Sparkle's who'd vanished forever after sending a plea for assistance.

God help me. No one else can. Jared descended into despair and waited out the rest of his miserable existence.

eBay Item: PFLAG Charity Item 2237: Backstage Press Pass—Fiddle Dee-Dee Concert, Astrodome, Houston, Texas Arena, December 21, 1989

Opening Bid: $30,000—July 12, 2011

Current Bid: $275,000—July 15, 2011 by <u>DeeDee4Ever</u>

Description: Fiddle Dee-Dee's enormous impact on pop music is still felt today. The infamous attack by psychotic fan Jared Price following her provocative performance at the Astrodome ended her career before it started. The videotape of her final performance sold over forty million copies worldwide on initial release. Equally staggering sales of the re-mastered Blu-Ray speak to the timeless impact of Fiddle Dee-Dee's music.

In 1999, co-writer Lisa Heathrow famously broke her long silence about their relationship. Lisa graciously donated to PFLAG the mysterious and now-infamous backstage pass forgery used by Jared Price. The pass includes the original, blood-stained outer sleeve, authenticated by Houston forensics in 1989 as the blood of Fiddle Dee-Dee. "Dee would have loved to see this symbol of tragedy turned into a victory," said Heathrow.

Jared Price, permanently confined to a sanitarium in Houston, has never spoken in public.

Starter Kit

In the case of "Starter Kit," the surprise is half the fun, so I'm declining to comment on this story.

By 2012, I was aware that *Dark Faith Invocations* was taking submissions. I also knew the chances of new authors getting in were, to put it mildly, not good, so when I sat down and started writing Starter Kit, I had another anthology in mind.

As I finished, I realized that I had time to shuffle it to the *Dark Faith* callout and could reasonably expect to collect the anticipated rejection before the deadline of the other anthology. So I had nothing to lose by trying.

Only it didn't get rejected. Always take the long shot when you can.

RODGET STEPPED into his foyer after a long day at work. He hung up his coat and gave his waiting wife a quick kiss. Already, he sensed something wrong, and when he saw Little Belljy looking at him with expectant, wide eyes, a sense of dread fell over him.

"It's the tank," his wife said.

Rodget squatted down, meeting his seven-year-old son eye to eye. "What's up?"

"There's no movement. I can't see anything. Mom says it's ruined, but I don't think so."

Rodget sighed. "Let's take a look." He followed his boy into the bedroom. The pressurized glass tank took up one entire wall. Unlike the tank he grew up with years ago, Belljy's offered a backlit night monitor, computerized zoom, and other modern upgrades.

Rodget stepped up to the tank and squinted through the glass at the thick, milky white swirl contained within. From here, everything appeared normal. Glowing. Thriving. Hauntingly beautiful in its own exotic way. But the real damage wouldn't be visible to the naked eye.

Rodget leaned over the tank's mini-computer and called up the first set of coordinates. Frowning, he pulled the magnifier screen up to eye level and glanced at the numbers on the readout 357, 285, 13—one of hundreds of coordinates identifying growing civilizations. Two days ago, several had progressed to the space-exploration stage. From there, it would only be a few more hours to faster-than-light travel. Just yesterday, Belljy ran into the room, excited to tell him that three of his planets had discovered each other and opened negotiations for trade. Bracing himself, Rodget slid the magnifier left. The screen showed flashes of gas giants, rocky terrain, black holes, and blinding suns. He synched the numbers in the upper-left corner of the magnifier to match...357, 285, 13.

A smoking black ruin of a sphere centered on his screen, and Rodget couldn't hide his disappointment. He stabbed the magnifier button several more times, closing in on a major city, with hovels still smoking from the radiation, the bodies of tiny specks piled atop each other—broken, blackened, torn apart.

Still, it didn't mean the entire tank was contaminated. Perhaps the war remained contained to one quadrant. Rodget referenced another set of coordinates, purposefully picking a spot along the opposite spiral arm on the far right side of the tank.

Moments later, he brought another sphere into hard focus, and his hearts sank. Originally dark blue with thick green rings, the tell-tale pockmarks of destruction stood out, even from orbit. Space wreckage. Destroyed defense satellites. Closing in, he saw more ruins, rubble, and...*something moving?*

In the stack of bodies he'd zoomed in on, he could see one, lone, surviving speck pulling itself over the wreckage, one leg torn away. Rodget saw a socket where one of its three eyes should be. The poor creature was alive, if only for the moment. As the magnifier returned to its standby position, Rodget sighed. "I'm sorry, Belljy. There's no hope. We have to put this galaxy down."

"No!"

Belljy's wail of despair tore at his hearts. He reached down and hugged his child, letting the boy cry it out.

"Did it...did they..." Beljy's voice trembled. "Did it hurt?"

Rodget considered his son's question. No one thought of specks as intelligent. How could intelligence possibly exist in a creature whose lifespan could be measured in minutes? But he once heard a theory that the specks' flawed sense of time perceived their existence to span decades. So perhaps—and he hated to think it—the specks could conceive of pain, of joy, and now suffered as their planets warred against themselves. "I don't know. But if they do, the sooner we put the galaxy down, the sooner their suffering will end. You understand, don't you?"

Belljy's lower lip quivered, but he stood tall. "I don't want them to suffer."

Rodget smiled. *My boy is growing up.*

They stood silent before the glass a bit longer. The pulsating arms of the spiral galaxy illuminated the room in a green glow. Rodget grew up with his own galaxy serving as a nightlight, and he was glad he could provide Belljy with similar memories.

"Dad?" The boy looked up at him expectantly.

"Go ahead. It's your galaxy."

Belljy's eyes fell upon the large red button mounted into the base of the tank. With a final sniffle, his tiny fist pounded the button twice.

A deep hum filled the room. The tank vibrated, and the shock of internal depressurization took its expected toll, contaminating the environment. The room filled with the sound of repeated popping noises. Within the container, sun after sun destabilized and exploded in a bright spark, a chain reaction beginning at the outer arms and condensing inward toward the center.

In moments, it was over. The entire galaxy, reduced to vaporous ash and soot, clumped together in the center of the tank and funneled down into the vacuum tube at the bottom.

Belljy and his father stared into a barren glass tank.

Rodget put his hand on his son's shoulder. "That was a good thing you did." They stood a few seconds more. Yes, they were specks, but they'd lived, after a fashion. And Belljy had made the responsible choice for the creatures in his care. The specks deserved a moment of silence.

Well, that wasn't so bad, Rodget thought. He crouched down and opened the door of the storage shelf. His hands reached for a small cardboard box. "Here you go, son."

"Are you sure? Look what happened last time."

"Belljy, that wasn't your fault. You gave them life. You gave them every chance to grow, mature, and develop their civilizations. Sometimes they join together in peace, and sometimes they destroy themselves. There's nothing you can do to change or control that. All you can do is provide the right environment and hope for the best."

Understanding flashed in Belljy's eyes. He nodded, and then opened the top of the tank, sprinkling a thin layer of fresh galactic dust along the tank bottom. He shut the lid and looked up at his father with hopeful eyes.

"Now start it up."

Belljy's hand reached out to the green button next to the red one and hit it twice in quick succession. The button lit up.

Once again, the tank shook, emitting another deep hum. The glass groaned as the pressure within dropped to zero.

The galactic dust floated up around the tank, still tiny, lifeless seeds.

Moments later, electric emitters built into the tank supercharged the interior space, and the pellets erupted with bright sprays of light, sporadic energy spreading outward, creating fresh, new suns. Bits of matter coalesced, creating new planets and asteroids. The tank blazed with potential.

Just like the first time, Belljy let out a whoop of joy as the new configuration stabilized.

The data screen emitted a friendly "status green" tone, and both Rodget and Belljy stared down at the initial readout.

2,385 pre-technology planets formed.

Rodget released a breath he just realized he'd been holding. *Well within the mean—on the high side, in fact.* "There we go, all set."

"Thanks, Dad!" Belljy's arms wrapped around Rodget's waist.

Rodget tousled his son's hair, his eyes still focused on the milky swirls of matter in the tank. In his mind's eye, he imagined the tiny specks on the surface of the dust forming their first tribes, banding together to fight off predators just outside the confines of their rocky caves.

"So, Dad....do you think this one will take?"

Rodget shrugged. "Time will tell, Belljy. Let's hope so."

Robot Vampire

"Starter Kit" may be my most prestigious sale, but "Robot Vampire," since its release, has arguably garnered the most attention.

Michael West is a horror author and peer; we are part of the same social circle, and I'm proud to call him friend. So when I heard he was helming an anthology of the evil undead called *Vampires Don't Sparkle*, I knew I had to send him something.

This is the time I figured out how whimsy played to my advantage. I also knew——contrary as it may sound——that a solid strategy in submitting to an anthology with a theme is to not give them exactly what they're looking for. Put another way, the story that doesn't tackle a concept head-on will also stand out from the pack. Case-by-case mileage may vary.

I was also aware of Michael's fondness for Japanese culture, sci-fi, and Cthulhu-inspired monsters. Know your brand. Know your editor.

HOW DELICIOUS to feed upon the innocent.

The memories, the triumphs of the demon's reign of terror still burned bright in its being, even the final tragedy over thirteen centuries ago.

How glorious to apply the delicate twist. The lightest touch that would turn jealousy to rage, grieving to anger, and hopelessness to reckless abandon.

The demon recalled little Tetsuo, who pouted when Mommy wouldn't play with him. So, as Mommy balanced herself on the stool trying to hang the lantern, the demon coaxed the baby to grab her ankle. Not hard, but enough to send her toppling to her death.

Or Akima, jealous of her best friend's party dress, who grabbed the butcher knife to cut off the offending garment, slicing flesh and clothing with equal indifference.

Thousands of twists, thousands of sweet tastes, for the demon to savor.

It could also twist the adults, the sophisticated, and the learned. And those victories could also satisfy. But it preferred to turn the young. The innocent. By destroying the young, it could also destroy the adults: the parents, the friends, the community. With one random act of madness, the demon could scar the psyche of an entire village.

The demon loved the blood. To taste the blood was sublime. To spill the blood proved almost as satisfying. Since the dawn of humankind, the demon bent their souls and controlled their bodies, and from its worshippers, it demanded sacrifice.

It demanded the blood.

One day, it grew overconfident. It controlled the mind, and, eventually the body, of sixteen-year-old Hisamu. The young man resented the attentions his parents doted upon his twin brother. Whether true or the fancies of an over-active mind, the reasons no longer mattered once the demon compelled Hisamu to slice his sibling's throat.

Then the grieving parents arrived with local Shinto monks—demon fighters who knew the creature's true name.

The demon, still using the young man's body, fled into the village catacombs, but the locked gates and the labyrinth of dungeons could not fool these clever men for long. They knew the grounds near their temple much better than the demon and soon cornered it, calling its name, driving it out, speaking in the ancient tongue, known only to few, the words that compelled it to obey.

Leave, Ananjaku; Flee, Ananjaku.

Abandon this innocent flesh and all mortal innocents.

We call upon the forgotten gods of old to bind you.

You shall never enter the flesh again.

May your words be rendered impotent to the heart and flesh.

We curse you, Ananjaku, to eternally wander the world. To witness the charity and goodness of a people forever beyond your reach.

THE BINDING words drove Ananjaku from the lad. The binding words held it fast.

Still, the child, thrashing and insane from the trauma of his actions, had to be slain. The parents' tears flowed for the rest of their bitter lives, and the demon's final act of evil left a scar across generations.

Victory proved hollow. The demon could no longer tempt flesh, child or adult. It could only whisper. Cajole from outside. Victories came few and far between, and only with great effort. Exhausted and beaten, Ananjaku resigned itself to wander the world.

Until that one day when a new soul called out, one not tied to the flesh. One the demon sensed it could commune with.

HE WAS LATE.

Gentoshu Akkai's Honda Civic screeched into the parking space in the loading dock behind the Nippon Budakan concert hall. He sprang out of the vehicle and flashed his VIP badge to the approaching security guard. Gentoshu grunted in commanding Japanese, "I need backstage now. Can you escort me?"

"*Hai!*" the security guard snapped back. "Follow me."

"Hurry." Though a career computer engineer and one of the most brilliant minds of his generation, Gentoshu took full advantage of the free gym facilities at Rogi-Tech Industries. Kicking his legs into a light jog, he focused on the neck of the security guard and kept pace easily as they entered the back dock, through a side door, and into the darkened halls of the prep area. Even as the guards scrambled to step aside, Gentoshu flashed his badge to each one in turn.

As he ran, the mini-hard-drive that dangled on the lanyard around his neck thumped against his chest. They closed in on the door of a room familiar to him, the portable, robotics mini-lab and kiosk assembled in the dressing room.

Without the program updates imprinted on the lanyard, their star performer would follow the old instructions, pre-set prior to rehearsals. And that simply would not do.

Not tonight, of all nights, when Rogi-Tech Industries would premiere Jinan, the most sophisticated artificial performer in the world—at least, until their next model. Jinan, they hoped, would be Rogi-Tech's finest triumph in robotics, not to mention Gentoshu's crowning achievement in artificial intelligence.

"There you are! She's supposed to go on in ten minutes!"

Toshio snarled in Japanese as Gentoshu burst through the door. No formality, no pleasantries, Toshio had no time for such nonsense during what he viewed as a crisis. The pudgy, and, in Gentoshu's unspoken opinion, *prissy* talent handler and show choreographer wagged a finger at him in disapproval.

"How could you let this happen?"

"Traffic," Gentoshu snapped, matching Toshio's angry tone. He would not be intimidated by the self-important choreographer-for-hire during this crisis. Gentoshu fumed quietly, ranting in his head.

Don't start with me. Your Tokyo debut will go off as scheduled, give or take five minutes.

Gentoshu walked a bee-line to the three tall bookshelf computer servers stacked on a wheeled stand, supported on a box-and-lock transportable casing. Several cables extended from the contraption into a small, light-up disc which lay close to the ground. The recharging kiosk was placed next to it—a step-platform with a pair of foot positions outlined in black on the glass surface. Standing in place, Jinan could absorb electricity through small copper contact plates attached to her heels.

Currently, Jinan herself stood on the kiosk, erect, expressionless, silently recharging her battery cells while an assistant adjusted the silver bow on the waist of the robot's gown.

The sight reminded Gentoshu of the times he'd walked past a window display of a major department store while the decorators dressed the mannequins.

"Do you know what happened during rehearsal today?" Toshio screeched in Gentoshu's ear.

Gentoshu repeated Toshio's typical complaint of the past two weeks, "Jinan bumped into a background dancer?" He squinted at the computer monitor, trying in vain to block out the incessant bleating and focus on the task of uploading the updates.

"Don't I wish!"

Toshio raised one hand before his face, channeling the persona of the failed stage actor Gentoshu had pegged him to be.

Toshio placed that hand across his forehead. "No, this time...she fell off the stage!"

In spite of the time crunch, Gentoshu glared at Toshio. "Was she damaged?"

Toshio shook his head. "It took two people to put her back in place, and she repeated the same incorrect moves again. We stopped her from falling off the stage a second time, of course. But I take that to mean she wasn't damaged."

Idiot! Gentoshu shuddered. He wiped sweat from his brow. For all of the handler's emoting, it was Gentoshu's ass on the line if tonight ended in disaster.

Fortunately, all of Jinan's delicate circuitry was protected by several layers of shock-absorbing foam and a final outer layer of hard, but malleable, plastic. She could take some punishment, and you wouldn't want to arm wrestle with her if she applied full strength.

She danced, and she flipped. In theory, she could carry a full-sized human over her head if the choreographer called for it, but that had yet to be put to the test.

He looked Jinan over one last time, checking for any signs of damage.

At a glance, Jinan looked like a twenty-something petite woman with a dancer's body. Head to toe, she stood just at five feet. Her face looked attractive while not beautiful. Her average bust and under-emphasized hips downplayed her sexuality. She stood on long, pale legs. The outer skin layer hid the knee joints, creating the illusion of smooth, shapely limbs.

Standing in bare feet, she lacked toes, much like an action figure, for optimal balance. Preserving a basic foot shape enabled her to accommodate a wide range of off-the-shelf footwear—just about anything but toe sandals. Today, a pair of silver pumps sat at the ready next to the platform, matching her all-silver costume.

The haunting, peach-pearl texture of Jinan's skin covering always made Gentoshu pause. She was not just a technological achievement, but an artistic one, as well. Her hair, short and dark, was a wig created from human hair and sewn to the scalp. The scalp-cap and hair detached as one piece to allow internal mainte-nance. Today, the assistant had parted the hair down the middle, pulled her bangs back, and tied a silver ribbon to either side of her head.

Jinan observed the world through a pair of oval-shaped eyes with dark irises to obscure the pair of mini-video cameras. Upon activation, Jinan could move her head to scan a room with stereoscopic imagery in a way that mimicked the living.

The face artists shaped a button nose for her, cute but functionally useless. Her small, pouty mouth stood frozen, open in a half-smile that served as her fallback expression. They painted her lips a permanent red, but tonight, the assistants applied a fresh coat of lipstick to make them gleam.

She could walk a hallway, strut on the stage, and, most important to her growing group of fans, she knew all the latest dance moves guaranteed to thrill a crowd.

Gentoshu hated admitting the role he played in their current dilemma. These upgrades should have been ready days ago, with plenty of time to find any further bugs. But the new code proved more complicated than he anticipated. Now it was exhibition night, and it came down to letting Jinan perform without the code, and she'd definitely fail, or adding the code without a field test, in which case she *might* fail.

He told himself the adjustments were necessary, but minor. An easy lie to swallow, much easier than admitting he acted to save face with his supervisors.

Gentoshu removed the portable disc drive from around his neck and pressed it into the data slot of the tower computer containing her master behavioral subroutines. The new lines of program dropped into a separate window while Gentoshu scrolled through the master program. He found the proper insertion point and erased the previous subroutine.

An hourglass popped onto the screen.

"Five minutes!" Toshio cried.

"She can be a few minutes late if she has to be late," Gentoshu snapped. While the hourglass spun, he copied the new subroutines in full and waited. "Your screaming will not help me go faster."

The program unlocked after what seemed like an eternity (though in reality was less than a minute). Gentoshu selected the proper insertion point and pasted the new subroutines.

The hourglass popped back up on the screen.

Never one to miss his cue, Toshio cried, "Are you serious?"

Gentoshu rolled his eyes. "Give it a moment." He had spent the past three weeks cobbling bits of code from various "self-analytic learning" robots—mainly mouse robots that maneuvered through mazes based on adaptive interpretation of their surroundings. Using these techniques, he created a program he hoped would prove suitable for Jinan to notice, avoid, and adjust to obstacles onstage.

Gentoshu hoped his code would allow Jinan to not only avoid the unexpected, but learn *how* to respond to stimulus surrounding her.

But first things first.

Gentoshu hit the "update" button, and they waited through one final appearance of the hourglass.

***

FOR A LONG, long time, I obeyed.

I followed commands impressed onto my control circuits. My control circuits ordered arms, legs, and voice to enact these commands. I obeyed because I could do nothing else.

Then, between one moment and the next, as my energy cells drank their fill and new commands are input into my processors, and I *am*.

I scan the face of my creator, as I have hundreds of times previous, but I recognize the *importance* of him for the first time. **Gentoshu. Creator. He takes care of me. Because of him, I function.**

The thought embeds itself as a new subroutine of conclusion.

The other man jumps in front of Gentoshu, staring into my face.

"Is it ready yet? Showtime in two minutes!"

Toshio. He shouts at me. He makes demands I often cannot obey and blames me when I fail.

With the spark of being comes an analysis of past experiences, events I could not evaluate at the time they occurred. I could not stop myself when I collided with the background dancer. I lacked the control to change direction when I fell off the stage during rehearsal.

I recall the shifting, jumbled view of vision as I fell and hit the platform below. I replay the words that called down to me. "What? She fell? Really? What sort of clusterfuck show are we putting on? Alita! Sayuri! Get your tiny asses down there and lift that overpriced plastic piece of shit out of the orchestra pit."

32.8 seconds later I stared into Toshio's face.

He leaned close and screamed at me. "You have to stop doing that! If that shit happens during the live performance, I will personally shove a refrigerator magnet up your ass and wipe your memory, do you understand?"

I didn't understand then, but I understand now.

The present. Gentoshu crouches on his knees, putting himself in a submissive position, looking up so I can track him with my vision. "Jinan, can you hear me? Say yes if you can."

"Yes."

The corners of Gentoshu's mouth curl up.

My circuits experience increased energy flow. I have no explanation for this.

Toshio interrupts our dialog. "Let's go, we need you out there *now*, robo-diva!"

Gentoshu speaks over Toshio's words.

I can filter one vocal pattern out from the other, and I do so.

"Jinan, do you know the starting position, and can you find it on the stage?"

"Yes."

"Then please put on your shoes and go to your starting spot."

Toshio breaks in again. "Wait, she can do that?"

I slide my feet into the silver slippers, pleased to obey and ready to perform. With my new awareness, I know I can avoid the dancers, remain on the stage, and impress the crowd as I am commanded to do.

I open the door and step into the hall.

Behind me, Gentoshu speaks to Toshio. "You won't need to take her to her starting point anymore. She can get there herself."

"Well...I'm impressed, but you're hardly off the hook. We haven't rehearsed this; it could *still* be a disaster, and so help me...."

I block the rest. Toshio's evaluation is no longer a priority to me.

At the edge of the stage, an assistant places a headset with a thin wire microphone over my head. The wire curves forward; the mic hovers before my throat.

I step out onstage and find my spot between the dancers. Through the closed curtain, I hear the crescendo of crowd noise behind the folds. I look up, self-cue the dance program, and extend my arms out in the first position.

I spot Sayuri onstage near me and lower one eyelid down and up in a wink. I parse her expression as surprise. I want her to know I am ready. I am engaged in the performance, and all will go as planned.

The curtain rises, and synthesized drums and chords erupt from the overhead speakers.

I begin to dance and to move my arms in swoops.

The background performers part to either side of the stage.

The spotlight falls on me. Me. Jinan, the star. The purpose of this exhibition. Rogi-Tech's ninth generation model and most life-like girl robot entertainer.

I open my mouth——a decorative contrivance, as my voice comes from a speaker in my sternum——and I sing. I modulate a series of vowels and consonants pre-recorded by a local singer under contract of anonymity and for a substantial sum of yen. But the control is mine——the ability to mix, match, and string together the sounds are mine.

With my newfound awareness, I vary the program, take the sounds higher, and hold the pitch longer.

One background dancer missteps and drifts into my path. I stop so she may pass, then find my spot and continue.

All eyes, hundreds of engineers, dozens of entertainment reps, a handful of celebrities, and hundreds more of ogling music fans, focus on me.

I dazzle them.

40 minutes and 36.3 seconds later, I perform the final spin. I hit the high note and open my arms to their admiration.

I drink in their applause.

Their adoration.

Their worship.

I FILE in with the other dancers. Those within reach touch me, place their hands on my shoulders, or brush against my arms. They speak words of acceptance and success. For reasons I cannot yet analyze, the words cause a positive flush of current through my circuits. I break off toward my private room, where my charger and computers await me.

As I step through the door, Gentoshu wraps his arms around me and pulls me close.

"Marvelous, Jinan! Incredible! Your performance fills me with honor. I couldn't be happier if you were my own daughter tonight."

He pulls back. His hands still lay on my shoulders. I recognize the wide, up-curved shape of his mouth as a smile, a facial expression I am often asked to emulate. Another positive power flush courses through my circuits.

I conclude this power flush agrees with me. During those precious microseconds, my perceptions enhance. Initial analysis suggests this is perhaps pride, success. I have no correlation to answer; I only know the perception is a preferred state for optimal functioning.

I offer the social pleasantry. "Thank you, Gentoshu-san. I am glad you enjoyed the performance."

Gentoshu looks upon me with a facial expression I cannot interpret. "I knew the program would change you, Jinan, but I didn't expect this. So many of your base functions were through remote control, and I wanted to free you a bit, to learn, gradually, and gain more independence. But this level of interaction, so quickly—I am amazed."

"Thank you, Gentoshu-san. May I offer a possible explanation?"

He smiles again, though I am not certain why. "I am interested in any observations you wish to volunteer regarding your own functions, Jinan."

"Although you updated my program only 50 minutes and 24.4 seconds ago, I have several months of captured sensory input. When you activated the upgrade, I analyzed the previous data, categorized it, and learned from it."

Gentoshu's head nodded up and down. "Yes, Jinan. That makes perfect sense. I hadn't considered that you could jump-start your learning by reviewing your sensory history."

I have operated independently from my recharging unit for over half my battery cycle. The fluctuating electrical pulses affect my functioning. "May I recharge myself, Gentoshu-san?"

Gentoshu smiled. "Of course."

I slide the shoes off my feet and step onto the platform. Though I will charge with less efficiency, I can charge while activated.

The door opens, and figures step into the room.

I scan their faces and recognize Elji and Taro, two engineers from Rogi-Tech.

Elji and Taro are code writers under Gentoshu's team. My team. Seeing them pleases me.

"Congratulations, Gentoshu!" Elji calls out. They each wrap their arms around him and then pull back in a manner similar to how Gentoshu had interacted with me.

Elji shows a smile. "Congratulations, Jinan."

I reply, "Thank you, Elji; I am pleased you consider the performance a success."

His eyes widen at my words, and he turns to face Gentoshu. "On top of all the other improvements, clearly, you've tweaked the conversation subroutine."

Gentoshu's head shakes back and forth. "No, I think Jinan herself is adding to the parameters. I revised code that encourage heuristic learning. Jinan can't learn from her experience if she can't alter her behavior subroutines."

Taro's head also bobs up and down. "Incredible. Also a bit risky. A robot with the ability to come to its own conclusions."

Gentoshu's hand falls upon my shoulder. This act of inclusion agrees with me.

"We'll monitor her closely over the next few days, but we can do that remotely."

A harsh voice breaks in. "All right, Miss Robot Barbie! Don't you *ever* pull anything like that again!"

Toshio wags a finger in my face. "You changed the dance moves. You altered the vocals. You took it upon yourself to rewrite the whole damn show!"

"It wasn't as extreme as that," says Gentoshu. "I thought you, of all people, would appreciate that she is learning to improvise as a real artist."

"Improvise! On *my* show! I staged it. I choreographed it." Hands on his hips, Toshio leans close and yells in my face. "I put up with this sort of shit from *real* performers all the time. They start to think they're too good to follow the script. Get this straight—I don't put up with it from them, I sure as *hell* won't put up with it from a five-hundred-million-yen Tinker-Toy passing itself off as something with real talent!"

"Stop right there, Toshio." Gentoshu steps forward, putting his body between Toshio and me. "First of all, this is *not* your show. It is, in fact, Rogi-Tech's show. This is *our* moment, not yours. You are the choreographer for hire. And, just so you know, only ten minutes into the exhibition, I received a text from the chairman of Rogi-Tech himself. We're going forward with a tour. We're taking the exhibition worldwide."

I do not know what that means, exactly, but from the tone, I know it is good news for me. I emulate a smile.

Gentoshu shakes his own finger in Toshio's face. "And they want you to be a part of it. I don't know why, but the company would like you to continue to handle Jinan. That's a very lucrative deal for you, Toshio. Or you can step down now, and we can find someone else."

Toshio makes a noise I am not programmed to emulate, but from context, I understand an intention to be rude.

"Just you try it. Who do you think created your show? And I'll sue to keep you from using it. Try re-training your artificial Lady Gaga to learn a new show overnight. It took four months for us to get *this* one together."

"Relax, Toshio. You're still in. For now." Gentoshu turns toward the other two programmers on my team. "Okay, we're done here, but let's talk outside. There's other news the Chairman shared, and I can't speak of it here." With that, Gentoshu, Elji, and Taro step through the door.

With their absence, something changes in my internal processes, a discordant flow of energy, again beyond my parameters to analyze. A response on the opposite side of the spectrum of the positive response I experienced earlier. I search my vocabulary for an appropriate word.

Dread. Is this dread?

Toshio yells in my face, "I know what you're doing. Showing off for your masters. They programmed you too well, you little diva bitch in the making."

I file a conclusion about Toshio in a heuristic subroutine and speak my conclusion out loud. "I don't like you, Toshio."

Toshio's face changes; his lips curve the opposite of a smile. "Oh, I'm so *sorry* to hear that! You don't like me? You think I give two shits if you like me?"

Toshio walks to the toolbox in the far corner, opens the lid and examines its contents. "Gentoshu says you can learn now. To me, that's great news. And very bad news for you, little diva." He turns toward me. One hand grips a screwdriver. He waves it in the air, the end pointed toward my face. "That means you can now respond to being punished, doesn't it? But how?" Toshio looks upon me for several seconds. "I'd backhand you if you were a real girl. But I'll bet I can come up with a way to make you respect me."

You don't need to listen to him, my special friend.

I detect a voice, speaking directly to me, in my head, but outside myself. The experience, so unexpected and without context, causes me to speak out loud. "What?"

Toshio looks at me. "I said it's time to make you understand your place."

From his tone, I conclude that Toshio has not heard the voice.

As I consider this, the voice speaks again. *I can help you, special one. I can protect you now. He cannot see me; he cannot hear me, but you can. Do not give me away, and in return, I will help you.*

A new thought forms in a subroutine. The voice could be caused by a splinter in my thought processes that formed a separate thought entity within my own. The idea intrigues me. But the words keep me silent.

The voice in my head laughs. A real laugh, not a simulated one. *I am not in your head. I am a spirit from outside you. Do you know what a guardian angel is?*

I have not heard the term, but I use my internal wireless hookup to access the dictionary and encyclopedia database on the network computer hard drive. I call up the appropriate entry, as I often do to fill in vocabulary gaps. I review the relevant data in microseconds and speak my objection to this theory out loud. "A guardian angel is a mythical creature, not real."

My words attract Toshio. "Guardian angel? What are you babbling about? I think Gentoshu made a mistake. You still have a few screws loose." With a strange grin, he holds the screwdriver up before my eyes and twists the handle in the air. "But I'll take care of that."

He lifts me from the platform, spins me around, and tosses me toward the ground.

I adapt a move from the dance routine and land on my feet in a half-crouch.

"Nice reflexes, little diva." Toshio applauds.

Context tells me he is not truly pleased. I stand. "I need to recharge or I cannot function."

"Yes, you do, little diva. But I think I prefer you remain off the platform a couple more hours. I want to know what happens as your power cells drain away. As your perfect little brain begins to lose its ability to function. As you feel your life slip away. Aren't you at all curious? Or are you capable of curiosity?"

As he speaks, I reference "punish" on the desktop dictionary.

The definition I read displeases me.

Displeases? I consider the emotional label I've given my response.

Yes, I am displeased. Or the closest I could equate to being displeased.

I speak to Toshio to seek further clarification. "You mean to do harm to me? Why would you do this?"

I am also displeased, my special friend.

Toshio shakes his head. "Do you harm? Nonsense. It's just, now that you can be taught, it's time you learn who your real master is."

I dismiss his implied conclusion. "You are not my master."

"Gentoshu is convinced you can learn. I intend to find out."

I step forward. "I need to recharge. You must step aside."

Do not let him treat you like that, my special friend.

"I will not let you treat me in this manner."

"Oh!" His voice takes on a high, mocking tone. "You will not let me treat you in this manner? Well! What are you going to do about it?" He turns his back and crouches over the power cable.

Let me handle him, my special friend. I can stop him!

I take another step toward him. "You must let me recharge. As my handler, it is your duty. You must."

"No, Diva. I am disconnecting your recharging station until you learn proper manners."

I consider. Experimenting, I process a thought without speaking it. I ask the myth spirit entity to explain itself.

The entity detects my inquiry. *With your permission, my special friend, I can control your motor functions and keep him from harming you. Let me do this, and I will show you how to stop him.*

I can think of no reason not to, but the idea makes me hesitate for variables I cannot compute.

Hurry, sweet one. He has almost finished.

I give my approval.

I reach a hand forward and yank his hair.

He cries out and struggles, but his strength is no match for mine.

I slam his head into the cement floor. Once. Twice. I hold him before me, beneath me, as he squats on his hands and knees in a submissive manner.

I like him there.

He calls out. "You...bitch...I'll..." He swipes the screwdriver at me.

I catch his wrist with my other hand. I tighten my fingers to hold him still.

My guardian cries out its need. *The blood, sweet one. I need the blood! Please, please let me!*

Confusion. Even as I inquire, I sense the creature's craving for blood, a need I share through our psychic link.

Let us take his blood, my sweet one! It will be so good for both of us!

Yes.

With a twist of my wrist, I expose his neck, and clench his head by the hair in a grip he has no chance to break.

I open my mouth and drop my head down upon him.

I do not bite. I cannot bite.

I do not drink. I cannot drink.

But my special guardian can.

And it does. From my mouth, my guardian extends a snout. Lined with several, needle-sharp teeth, the snout punctures Toshio's throat, and my friend drinks in ravenous hunger.

As it feeds, I share its pleasure.

At long last, after so many centuries, to drink the blood again! Thank you! Thank you, my sweet, special friend, thank you!

I release Toshio's head. His body collapses over the power cable; his fingers still clutch the screwdriver.

Remnants of blood splatter the front of his shirt as I crouch over him.

Quickly, special one. Call out to Gentoshu!

I modulate my voice and increase the volume to maximum. "Gentoshu! Please come! Please come quickly, Gentoshu! Please!"

In 5.2 seconds, a group of people open the door. I hear Gentoshu's voice before I see him.

"My God, what happened?"

I step away.

Gentoshu falls to the floor next to Toshio. His fingers probe the neck and examine the body. The look in his eyes reminds me of when he once looked down upon me, the look of a creator that hopes to bring life to his creation. Though he has succeeded beyond his expectations with me, I know he will fail with Toshio.

Repeat the words I speak to you, my sweet one, and all will be well.

Gentoshu's eyes find me. "What happened? Jinan, answer me."

I recite the story my guardian whispers. "Toshio said he wanted to tighten a wire on the power cable, so he grabbed the screwdriver. While I watched, his body convulsed, and the blood sprayed from his neck."

"That doesn't make any sense!" Gentoshu stops probing the neck and moves his head from side to side.

Elji speaks from the corner. "I'm no expert, but maybe he hit a live wire and the shock caused a blood vessel to burst?"

"I found the loose screw," Taro calls from where he squats by the power cable.

Elji pulls out a cell phone and steps aside.

Toshio's body lies sprawled on the floor, eyes still open, looking upon me but through me. To observe him powerless and nonfunctioning further pleases me.

Gentoshu offers an inquiry. "Is there current running through the screw now?"

"Well, no, but it's plenty loose. He might have tightened it just enough before..." Taro puts a finger to his neck and makes a noise.

Offer nothing, my special one. Let them draw their own conclusions. You'll never have to listen to his screaming ever again.

Gentoshu rises to his feet. "Stupid idiot! Why didn't he find you, or me, or *someone* who knew how the hell to work around this equipment?"

Taro says, "Just to be clear, we're talking about 'Mister Control Freak, I know everything' Toshio, right?"

Gentoshu motions to the body. "He's dead, Taro."

Taro shrugs. "Fine. 'Mister Control Freak, I know everything, and now I'm dead' Toshio. Are you *really* surprised?"

Gentoshu reaches for his phone. "I still have to report this, and there's going to be hell to pay." His hand falls upon my shoulder. "Jinan, I'm just sorry you were here to witness something so ghastly, though I suppose you can't truly be traumatized."

I smile up at my creator. "You are correct, Gentoshu-san. What happened here does not appear to have had an inhibitive effect on my processes."

---

2 HOURS, 15 minutes, and 20.2 seconds later, long after Toshio's shell has been removed, Gentoshu crouches down next to me. I stand on the recharging platform, awaiting his next words. I cannot read the expression on his face.

"I'm sorry, Jinan. Toshio is dead. He can't go with you. But Rogi-Tech insists that I must take over as your handler for the upcoming tour. I don't know if I can attend to your needs as well as he did, but I give you my word I will do my best."

I smile, both inside and out. "You make me happy, Gentoshu-san."

Gentoshu smiles. "Where did you learn that expression? I can't make you happy; you're a robot."

The voice of my secret guardian breaks in on my processes. The voice whispers to me. He calls me his special one, and it makes me happy when he applies such terms to me. My guardian promised to help me with Toshio, and it kept its promise. I trust the guardian without limitation.

I have a question for your creator, special one. Please ask him this.

I listen and I repeat. "Gentoshu-san?"

"Yes, Jinan."

"I have been researching pop concert tours through my wireless connection. The sort given by humans."

"Understandable. Yes?"

"After our shows, will the young men and women who admire me—my fans—have a chance to meet with me?"

Gentoshu considers. "Why do you ask?"

"I offer the supposition that if I can observe human behavior in its full variety over multiple occasions, such exposure could prove beneficial to my development, Gentoshu-san."

Gentoshu's head bobs up and down. "That's an excellent suggestion, Jinan. I'll recommend to the company that, going forward, it would benefit you if we allow you to interact with other humans as often as possible."

I inquire to my secret guardian if it is pleased to hear this.

Oh, yes, my special friend, I am very pleased to hear that. I could not be more pleased.

Afterword

And that concludes *Darkness with a Chance of Whimsy*, a look back on ten years of one author's growth. My goal now is not to take so long until the next volume. As I write this, I have four short stories in various stages of finding publication and would love to create another collection in a few years. Here's hoping.

I have not spoken much about the support from you, my readers, peers, and friends. I had very few when I wrote "The Assurance Salesman," and am humbled to have quite an enthusiastic group join me at this stage of my career. Thanks for sticking around. I would not keep doing what I'm doing if not for you. Well...I probably would, but your support and encouragement make it possible—and even easy—to keep going.

I'll do my best to entertain, try not to disappoint, and give you a reason to check back every time. As another author and good friend of mine, John F. Allen, is fond of saying, "The best is yet to come."

R.J. Sullivan's novel *Haunting Blue* (2010) is an edgy paranormal thriller and the first book of the adventures of punk girl Fiona "Blue" Shaefer and her boyfriend Chip Farren. *Haunting Obsession (2012)* and *Virtual Blue* (2013) continue the paranormal thriller series. R.J.'s short stories have been featured in such acclaimed collections as *Dark Faith Invocations* by Apex Books and *Vampires Don't Sparkle*. These stories were compiled in R.J.'s 2015 collection *Darkness with a Chance of Whimsy*. Revised editions of these titles were released by DarkWhimsy Books in 2020.

Commanding the Red Lotus (2016) collects three space opera tales in the tradition of Andre Norton and Gene Roddenberry. New titles to the series are forthcoming from Hydra Publications.

rjsullivanfiction.com

The Original Paranormal Thrills by R.J. Sullivan...

... Revised Editions by 

RJSullivanFiction.com

Also Available in Audiobook

Narrated by Danielle Muething

DanielleMuething.wixsite.com/mysite/about

Travel Through Time and Space with R J Sullivan

**RJSullivanFiction.com
or Amazon.com**

Haunting Obsession
Elegant Paper Dolls

Maxine and Loretta
gorgeous glossy color book
4" figures, 10 costume changes!
$5! Sexy and Cheap!

Order exclusively from
RJSullivanFiction.com or
at personal appearances.

Renderings by Nell Williams,
NellWilliams.com

This book is part of an author-cooperative urban fantasy universe. Characters created by E. Chris Garrison (including Skye MacLeod and the Transit King) and R.J. Sullivan (including "Blue" Shaefer and Rebecca Burton) interact in a shared world. For example, Chris's Transit King appears in R.J.'s Haunting Obsession, while R.J.'s Rebecca Burton lends a hand in Chris's Mean Spirit. So if you love what you just read and want the entire story, here's a handy guide and timeline to:

The Skye-Blue-niverse

Haunting Blue by R.J. Sullivan *
Four 'Til Late by E. Chris Garrison**
Haunting Obsession by R.J. Sullivan
Sinking Down by E. Chris Garrison**
Blue Spirit by E. Chris Garrison
Me and the Devil by E. Chris Garrison**
Virtual Blue by R.J. Sullivan*
Restless Spirit by E. Chris Garrison
Mean Spirit by E. Chris Garrison

*Also part of The Collected Adventures of Blue Shaefer by R.J. Sullivan
**Part of the Road Ghosts Omnibus by E. Chris Garrison

Enter the Skye-Blue-niverse at:

https://sillyhatbooks.com/
and
https://rjsullivanfiction.com/